Chester's Last Stand

Chester's Last Stand

A NOVEL BY

RICHARD E. BROWN

UNIVERSITY OF NEVADA PRESS

RENO & LAS VEGAS

*The paper used in this book meets the requirements of
America National Standard for Information Sciences—
Permanence of Paper for Printed Library Materials,
ANSI Z39.48-1984. Binding materials were chosen for
strength and durability.*

University of Nevada Press, Reno, Nevada 89557 USA
Copyright © Richard E. Brown 1988.
All rights reserved
Printed in the United States of America
Design by Richard Hendel

Library of Congress Cataloging-in-Publication Data

Brown, Richard E., 1946–
  Chester's last stand.

  I. Title.
PS3552.R6978C45   1988   813'.54   88-10659
ISBN 0-87417-138-5 (alk. paper)

To Larry,

with thanks

Chapter One

Both those strange allies, Chester and the new Methodist preacher, Selkirk, arrived in Hickman in the late spring after the planting—an act of real faith in the desperate dust bowl years—had been finished. They breezed into town separately and by different means, the preacher jammed into his sputtering old Model A, up to his neck with portmanteaus and spindly chairs, while Chester tumbled from a boxcar, seemingly at random, when some freight on its way to Chicago stopped to take on water at our depot. Still, the coincidence of their arrivals is notable, for both men were running from envenomed furies at their tails and both, when they beheld the ragamuffin children and the old geezers hanging around in front of the Hickman seed store, must have smiled in self-congratulation. Never mind the dust and the baking sun that hung perpetually over the town; something about the hot, thorny land and the hayseed faces told them both the same message: the odds were better here. It might be possible to recover. Among the clouds of powdery black soil that danced in corners, or maybe beneath the faintly greening hedges along the highway, who knows but what a sharp-eyed fellow might stumble onto some manna early in the morning and pluck it up like a silver dime before the natives had shuffled out of bed? Who knows but what a clever stranger might shake a little place like this until it settled into his personal promised land?

Which may sound like a fantastic dream, considering that there was poverty enough in Hickman then to rival the hobo jungles that grew up around the great switching yards in the cities. The best any reasonable person might say was that in northern Missouri, in the pocket where Hickman lay, the dust storms never blew quite fiercely enough to drive families out the way they were scourged from Oklahoma or Texas. Even so, there'd been some weeks of black blizzards and some days of grasshoppers, cattle had succumbed, Henry Wallace had ordered the farmers to slaughter their baby pigs to raise pork prices, and you could read it all in the hollow cheeks of a little girl, whining because her daddy didn't have the where-withal to buy ice cream on their weekly trip into town. Her old man, standing by the feed store, made a sheepish, bluster-ing joke to his idle companions about the greed of spoiled children. That was a dodge even noble men resorted to in the late thirties. Nevertheless, to Chester, who was used to the sight of breadlines stretching a dozen blocks, Hickman looked prosperous and even serene. Its dark old trees offered shade to a traveler, there was plenty of room for a man to stretch his arms as he walked along, and the housewives still had money for hocks and beans, if Chester's nose was any judge of the kitchen smells he passed.

The sight of hobos wandering about the town was rare then, despite the presence of a rail line connecting Chicago with the West Coast. Maybe once or twice some poor soul riding a freight in from the Rockies jumped off for a drink and a look around, but usually he didn't linger. He wanted to go on being poor, if that's what life had dealt, in the manner he'd grown used to, among comrades who shared his specific com-plaints and his knowledge of the road. But as Chester always boasted later, "I'm a man in a thousand!" and the first proof is that he took one look up and down the windblown streets of our little burg and decided to try his luck.

A second testimony to his grit is that once he'd made his decision to stay, no rebuff discouraged him. How he made his pitch for a job or a charity piece of pie, after knocking at all the back doors of Hickman, and how the women or even the children turned him away, he never mentioned to me in after years. That's not the sort of story Chester would tell on himself, it being no tribute to his powers. But he does seem to have gone through the town systematically, probing every possible opening and nearly starving in the process, without, in the end, finding any nook he could insinuate himself into. If, during that hungry week, he knocked at the Methodist church in hopes of a merciful handout to tide him over, the Reverend Selkirk probably frowned and turned him away just like everybody else—for how could the preacher have guessed that within three months his fate and Chester's would become so closely intertwined? However, the remarkable thing is that when any other drifter might have finally admitted his mistake and trudged back to the depot to wait for a freight, Chester still had enough gumption to start walking the rutted roads that stretched off from Hickman into the parched countryside, to see if he could get a foothold by hiring himself out as a farmhand.

That's how he stumbled onto the west county road and encountered my grandfather, Jake Calder, who was down at the barn doing his morning chores. Grandpa was still a young man in those days, strong as an ox, according to the tales I've heard, but gentle, trusting, and a perfect Christian, as my great-uncles used to say with the barest edge of sarcasm. Anyway, Chester must have presented a likely sight for Grandpa's compassion that morning. When Grandpa told the story about his first sight of the stranger, he always began, "This fellow looked as if he was going to offer himself to be planted for a scarecrow. He dragged himself up the driveway all covered with dust, his shirt was torn, he hadn't shaved in a week. Every bone in his face showed. You should've seen the way his skinny arms flew around, like they were puppet's limbs jangling. Nearly useless for work. They'd jerk up and circle his ear one minute, then flop down to his leg the next."

Maybe Chester looked so loose-limbed because he was fanning himself from the heat, or trying to dry out the stench of his armpits so he'd smell more agreeable, or maybe he was so exhausted that he'd lost control of his parts by then. But considering what everybody found out about his character in the months to come, the likelier truth is that every time he stepped on another sharp stone in the road he sought to fly above the pain, waving his arms like wings, hoping to out-soar his misery and get up to the happy golden days he'd de-cided were waiting for him hereabouts.

Anyway, Chester's grit appealed to my grandpa, who lifted him up and took him to the kitchen door, where he told my Grandma Agnes, "Give this stranger a plate of ham and eggs and all the left-over biscuits, and let him scrub himself under the pump."

Of course my grandmother wasn't so much a Christian as a Wilson, sister to the Wilson brothers that lived farther up our road, so she had different ideas about tramps who walked in smelling like a dung heap. Two biscuits and coffee is all the breakfast Chester got, though Grandpa didn't suspect any-one would behave so cruelly and had gone back to the barn, leaving Chester defenseless.

Grandpa was poor enough that he couldn't see his way clear to support a hired hand. Besides, he already had my father to help him with the farm, and anybody alive in those days knew your own thirteen-year-old boy is worth more than any stranger, unless you can watch over him every min-ute of the day. So after a few tasks to work off his biscuits, Chester was sent up the road to find his lunch elsewhere, Grandpa calling out, "God's richest blessing on you!" as the skinny fellow stumbled away. Grandpa was not too worried about him, however, since he'd explained to Chester that his four brothers-in-law lived within the next couple of miles, one farm adjoining the next, and two of those farms were un-usually large for our part of the country, so there was a good chance one of the brothers-in-law might want to take on an extra man.

Even if they wouldn't hire him permanently, Chester figured, each of those brothers should be good for one or two meals, and not every housewife on the road could be two-biscuit stingy.

Now, when Chester struck out for that first white frame house that stood atop the hill just west of Grandpa's, shadowed by a grove of elms and maples, it was the parting of the cunning from the guileless, and it was with the hope that Chester's smell for opportunity among the hayseeds had not betrayed him after all. A little determination was going to be rewarded at last with milk and honey. On the other hand, my sweet, sainted grandfather often shook his head when he told me about Chester's beginning. "If I'd known what lay ahead for old Chester among the Wilsons, I'd have driven him into town myself and shoved him into a boxcar headed for Illinois. Whatever he ran into there, it would've been better than sending him into that family of vipers."

But on a couple of occasions as he remembered those long-ago days, Grandpa also smiled, which even a Christian couldn't entirely help when he thought about Chester, and once he added, in an Old Testament mood, "You know, sometimes God sends the innocent to punish the guilty, but other times He just throws the guilty together to torment one another."

The rest of Chester's first week has taken on the status of legend in our family. I must have heard some reference to it twice a month during my boyhood, even though the events were already three decades in the past by then. Like all good yarns this one has been embroidered, sometimes told for pure comedy, other times for its moral value, or even reduced to proverbs, like "His feet were dragging just like Chester's that first day he came up our road." Of course Chester ended up lame in the left thigh where the muscle never healed properly, so when I say that this story has been told for comedy you must understand the particular flavor of the laughter.

My Great-uncle Claude and Aunt Kate, living atop the hill to which Chester first aspired, were the eldest members of the family, so Claude had inherited a double portion of land, two quarters or 320 acres, along with the original house my great-grandfather had built when he homesteaded, while the other three brothers and my grandma had each received a single quarter. Not that Uncle Claude, despite his age and honors, ever claimed to be the head of the family. If the Wilson councils did not operate as a democracy, at least all the brothers would have protested to an outsider that they did. Still, my Uncle Claude did claim one special inheritance from his father besides the double portion of land, and that was what we called the gift of gab.

So when he saw this thin figure in the dusty black city trousers and the flopping shoes shamble in from the road with half a hopeful grin knotted on his face, Claude didn't sic the dogs on him. He set down the bucket he was carrying and waited, leaning in the shade of the barn. He had plenty of leisure to notice that every time the newcomer stepped on a pebble, his brave grin wrenched into a grimace and both arms flew up beside his head in arcs. Uncle Claude turned his bucket upside down, settled his rump on it, and awaited the arrival of this promising spectacle.

When Chester got close enough Claude called out, "Welcome, stranger!" though he never did invite Chester to sit down but kept him, by a kind of jovial prodding, standing at attention. The bucket Claude sat on was placed so that anybody who stood before him was forced to squint into the sun in order to seek out his face, which floated cool and smiling but not completely visible in the intense shadow cast by the barn. By this time it was early afternoon, and as Claude chatted on, asking an occasional question and blending in the answers he received with observations about crops and weather and trains ("Have you ever ridden one, stranger?") and cows ("Did you ever milk one?"), the sweat dropped off Chester's long nose and made a black stain in the dust between his feet.

Claude had two sons himself, one of them a couple of years older than my father, so the work of the farm went on in the background while he talked. He wasn't worried about that. But finally the shadow from the barn that had been creeping up Chester's legs reached his shirt, and Claude could see that if he kept on talking it would pass over the stranger's nose at last, so when Chester finally blurted out, in a voice between a croak and a groan, "Your neighbor Mr. Jake sent me over to see if you needed an extra hand," Claude took up the suggestion quickly enough. He was ready to get on to the next stage of his game.

Now, any of the Wilson brothers, who had lived on farms all their lives, could tell if another man knew anything about farming by the way his muscles had formed or by the way he talked. Here Chester gave himself away every time he opened his mouth, as he pointed out the most commonplace things which any man of the soil would take for granted. "I see you got a weathercock perched on your barn roof. I see you sit on a galvanized pail." So Claude knew what he was dealing with, and when he thought of city fellows he didn't think of sophistication or superiority; he knew he was master over them without question.

Claude eased up from the pail and hitched his overalls and put his hand on Chester's shoulder as if in friendliness. He said, "I got one chore you could do that'd be good for a supper and a night sleeping in my hayloft." Then, magnanimously, he added, "Help yourself to the dipper that hangs by the well first, if you want." Finally he gave his instructions, and Chester shambled off to do the job.

Down at the bottom of the hill on the other side from

Uncle Claude, the identical white frame houses of my Great-uncle Tony and Great-uncle Jethro face each other like mirrors; only Tony's wife, my Aunt Liza, used to hang her wash on a line across the front yard, a practice which her sister-in-law (and sister, but that's another story), Aunt Vera, thought a bit indecent, so she strung *her* laundry line behind the house. And the trees in the yards were different, because the two brothers had figured out that the way the sun hit, one of them needed to plant for shade while the other could plant for fruit. They shared the shade from Tony's big trees all summer, and in the fall they divided Jethro's plums and apples and pears. Just like they had shared the sisters, and like they were going to divide up Chester as if he was a wedge of pie.

What with fatigue and the ferocious sun and the cruel gravel on the road, it was mid-afternoon by the time Chester turned into Jethro's drive. He had not yet eaten dinner, for Claude had promised to reward him *after* he'd completed the chore. Aunt Vera, Jethro's wife, was sitting under an apple tree beside her house, surrounded by a tangle of children and dogs, doing her mending and resting her legs before she had to go into the stifling kitchen and stoke up the stove for supper. The children fell silent and the dogs growled at the sight of a stranger, who stood at a respectful distance and asked, "Could I speak to Mr. Jethro Wilson, if he's at home?"

Vera snorted in that disparaging way she had. "You just passed him on the road."

Chester turned and saw a distant figure following a horse across a field. He must have passed within fifty feet of Jethro, but he had set his eyes toward that cool-looking white house within its circle of trees and had not heard plow cutting through soil or leather harness creaking on horse's back. Chester perhaps cursed himself, but to Vera he asked, "You through with Mr. Claude's goat? He sent me to fetch it."

Vera's needle slowed for a second and then without raising her head she sniffed, "You'll have to ask my husband about that."

The perfection of her reply was instinctive. She could not have guessed what lay behind the question, yet she thought enough like the Wilsons not to act surprised by anything. How many country wives would have asked, "What goat?" and after that the joke would have been lost! It was simple prudence on Vera's part, you might say, that she played so close to the vest. But she'd also taken in Chester's woebegone figure with one glance and had noticed that he'd walked about as far as a man could on such a smothering day if he was not well fed. So just like her brother-in-law Claude, she spoke the words that forced Chester to walk another quarter-mile. Being a woman and not caring to claim that she had been blessed with any gift of gab, however, she didn't bother to offer the stranger the water dipper that hung by the kitchen door; she just clammed up. Finally Chester muttered, "Thanks!" and turned toward Jethro in the field.

"Am I through with his what?" Jethro demanded, angry at being interrupted in his plowing. Chester hadn't enough experience to stand at one point on the edge of a field and wait for the horse to bring Jethro around again, but had tagged after him over the furrows, stumbling once or twice on some clods and not minding the young corn plants in his way. Jethro bellowed at him as though he was a darned fool, then clucked to the horse and called out over his shoulder, "Anything about a goat's between my brother and me."

Now desperation conquered Chester's exhaustion, for he knew that without that goat he'd get no supper. So he hurried up behind, flapping his arms and shouting back, "Mr. Claude says he's got a heap of tin cans that need to be eaten and he'd like his goat back by tonight and he sent me to fetch him."

Jethro pulled the horse up again and made Chester repeat

the business about the tin cans. Then he smiled. Because although he made no claim to the gab himself, he was not slow to understand, and he seldom failed to rise to an occasion.

"Oh, he finished all my cans this morning," Jethro said. "Then I passed him on to my brother Tony, that lives across the road." He gestured toward the identical house beneath the shade trees. "Tony'll be through with him by now, so you should be able to pick him up all right over there." As Jethro saw the fatigue and hunger and near-despair creep over Chester's face, he added, "But it won't do any good to ask at the house, because Tony's working out in his back forty this afternoon, and the missus won't give up the goat unless her man says to." Then Jethro stretched out his arm to indicate a hedgerow near the horizon, and a rise of ground beyond that. "Look on the other side of that rise," Jethro told Chester. The heat was shimmering in waves above the road.

About four-thirty Chester reached the top of the rise. He could see no one working in the field beyond. Far back at my Uncle Tony and Aunt Liza's barn, some small human shapes were pointing out the stranger to one another, and Chester cupped a skinny hand around his ear to catch the voices that blew toward him on the wind. But it was all a faint clamor lost in the rolling pasture he had just crossed.

Suddenly Tony saw the stranger sink down on the hilltop. Tony didn't yet know why he was there or what was wrong with him. My uncle had work to do and he plodded about the barnyard doing it, confident that the stranger would have to come in eventually, and then he'd see. Meanwhile Chester passed out, or dozed. At last Aunt Liza sent one of her children to ring the dinner bell. The sun went down. The family, tired from their labor, went to bed. In all this time, Chester did not stir from the hilltop.

Next morning, though, he was waiting on the kitchen step when Tony looked out shortly after dawn. Chester had taken off his shoes and was airing his feet patiently. He must have found the dew refreshing, or else he'd run across something edible in the barn, because he looked cocky enough and was able to force a grin. The way Tony told it, he noticed this stranger was suspiciously pleasant, and he wondered what he'd stolen.

Anyway Chester had enough hope left in him that he started in on Tony the minute he saw him. "Great weather you got around here!" he said brightly, as if he'd forgotten the parched look of the land and yesterday's withering heat.

It took a few minutes for Tony to comprehend such stupidity. Meanwhile Chester, as he went on spinning compliments out of the air, noticed that the other man wasn't grinning back yet or offering him any plate of hominy and peach pie. He realized that no breakfast was guaranteed to anybody just because he sat on Tony's back step with his shoes off, ready to speak a cheerful word. So Chester drew out his one resource. He said, "I've come for Mr. Claude's goat that eats the tin cans."

That made another stupid thing that the stranger had said. Tony burst out, "You're a fool and a liar! You're a no-good trespasser and a sidewinding thief!" He kicked Chester in the rump and started driving him toward the road with threats about the sheriff.

Chester leaped away fast enough to avoid the worst bruising, but then he walked backwards and tried to reason with Tony. His hopes were still high, if only he could convey to this thick-witted farmer that his mission was legitimate.

By shouting out the names of Claude and Jethro, Chester finally turned Tony's violence aside. Though Tony was outraged that a stranger would try to sell him such a cock-and-bull story, he began to wonder if Chester might be the intended dupe rather than himself. Tony wasn't natural at the gab like his brother Claude, but like Jethro he was sensitive to an opportunity.

At last he motioned Chester back. He mumbled a few

words that an inexperienced listener might mistake for apology. Chester nodded with a look he hoped didn't appear too clever, because he supposed that this hick was about to fall into his hands. Tony asked him to repeat his request and then pretended to understand: "Oh, so that's it! Claude wants *you* to take the goat back!"

Chester smiled toothily.

"But I haven't got him now," Tony said. "Last evening one of my other brother's kids came for him. They've been using tin cans all week like they were going out of style and needed them eaten up, so I passed him on."

Chester braced himself and asked, "You mean I can fetch the goat at Mr. Jethro's across the road?"

Tony shook his head. "I'm talking about my other brother, Alistair, that lives a mile farther down the road."

Chester could see what the morning held for him, and, facing in imagination a return of yesterday's fatigue and hunger, he dropped a hint. "Must be near breakfast time around here."

"I always milk before I eat," Tony replied. "But you can count on getting to Alistair's just as they sit down to table."

There was nothing for Chester to do but pull on his shoes and set out.

Here was a fellow so green that every time he stepped on a pointed stone, he must have looked down to see if he'd stumbled on one of those solid metal berries the goat had dropped on its way to a new supply of tin cans . . . But an even more accurate idea of Chester at this early point in his struggle with the Wilsons might be given by remembering those old animated cartoons in which a seedy tomcat strolls into town, whistling and twirling his whiskers, clad in a pair of overalls covered with bright red patches, hoping for a fish head. That tomcat wins your respect too, for the force of life in him, even though you've seen enough cartoons to know that within a few frames some pixie-faced mouse is going to hammer the cat's toe with a mallet and all the nasty kids sitting around you are going to chortle. That's the kind of inevitability we're dealing with here. I've already said something about the cruelty of the laughter.

Chester arrived at Alistair's place as his wife, my Great-aunt Sophie, was dishing up breakfast. Alistair didn't rise from his chair at the kitchen table, but called to the stranger through the open door. As Chester put his question about the goat he smelled the eggs and bacon, the biscuits and coffee, and a kind of fried mush that my family liked.

But Alistair only narrowed his eyes and stopped chewing long enough to answer, "I haven't got any goat. What would I want a goat for?"

Chester told him. Politely, for the odor of food was heavy. The family, assembled at the table, snorted and fell silent to see what Alistair would reply. Alistair had a bit of gab to him, if not quite as much as Claude, so he turned and looked carefully at Chester for the first time. He perceived the desperation as well as the foolish hope that had propelled this skinny wraith so far. It occurred to him that the Wilsons wouldn't get another day's entertainment out of the fellow if they didn't stake him to a few bites of grub. So Alistair called to his serving girl, Lindy, "Fix up a plate and pour another cup of coffee." Chester licked his lips.

A wistful lass of sixteen or seventeen appeared in the doorway with the food. In the light of morning Chester saw that she had a wondrous fresh milky complexion and auburn hair trailing to her shoulders. Blue eyes. She was wearing a shift made from chicken feed sacks, the kind with floral prints that farm wives saved for their children's blouses or for aprons. Her feet were pink and rounded like the backs of mice.

Lindy didn't bother to look at Chester, but set the plate and cup down on the step. The moment passed like a dream. Chester stared boldly now into the dark kitchen after her, but all he could make out was Alistair at the head of the table, wolfing down mush. Chester barely noticed, in his distraction, that there were only two dry biscuits on the plate. He found that his coffee had been heavily sugared and he sipped it longingly, for it seemed to taste like the girl. He didn't recover until Alistair pushed back from the table and stood over him, hoisting his overall straps over his shoulders in preparation for the day's work.

"That goat isn't here now," said Alistair, gazing off past the barn. "He ate up our tin cans by bedtime last night, so we put him out on the back eighty. I just got me a new piece of land last winter"—Alistair was congratulating himself on his holdings now, so he took a minute to tell Chester this detail—"that I'm beginning to work. There's a lot of scrap metal on it"—here he lapsed back into the necessary fiction—"that I need cleaned up. If you can wait, that goat'll be through around dinner time, and you can fetch him back to Claude."

At the mention of dinner Chester said, "Sure, I can wait."

Then Alistair asked, "What you doing this morning? You ever stand behind a plow?"

Chester didn't hesitate, for he smelled an opportunity and his cleverness overtook him. "Why, I been plowing since I was a little tyke! I plowed up most of the state of Iowa at one time or another, sometimes just for fun!"

Alistair allowed that his new eighty acres were hard to handle in addition to his already established farm, especially since none of his boys was big enough to hitch a team or follow a plow. "I'd give a man a good meal for a morning's work," he said.

Now Chester knew that his determination was about to pay off at last. Alistair led him to the barn, showed him the horse and the implement, and pointed to a nearby field.

Of course Alistair knew by all those crazy signs Chester wasn't aware of that this fool had never worked on a farm in his life. So as he left the barnyard he locked the gate to make sure the horse didn't escape while Chester was trying to hitch it to the plow. I should point out how risky this joke was. People have died from a kick by a horse. But I can only theorize that Alistair pursued his prank in order to act out a fantasy, for he *did* want another hand about the place—the extra eighty acres had been a mistake, and if they hadn't fallen into his lap for next to nothing he wouldn't have bothered to acquire them. Still, Alistair had this quality—related to the gab, I believe—of flinging himself into the arms of fate and daring to see what might happen to his advantage. That's the spirit in which he greeted Chester's claim that he knew how to plow.

After Alistair left it didn't take long for a sound of agony to come from the barn. Chester shrieked so loudly he was heard up at the house, causing my Aunt Sophie to send one of her boys down to find out what had happened. The child, Rudy, peeked betweeen two boards and saw Chester holding his knee and cursing, while the horse stood in a far corner, twitching its shoulder muscles. The boy ran back and told his mother, who smiled and said nothing.

But there were no more shrieks after that. Chester intended to be a survivor, and he made quick strides in learning how to handle an animal. He figured that if you couldn't treat a horse like a piece of machinery, maybe you could get it where you wanted with an encouraging pat on the neck. By ten o'clock the miracle had happened. The horse was hitched without anybody telling Chester the first thing about it. What did upset Alistair a bit was that Chester had no idea how to get from the barn to the cornfield with the equipment, so he just plowed a furrow across the barnyard to his destination. Fortunately, Alistair had the Wilson sense of humor and digested that as a joke by fate against himself. But mainly he was impressed with what Chester had achieved, and now he decided that he might actually get some work out of this stranger at a very low rate. He followed the new furrow out to the field where Chester was weaving around behind the plow, ready to offer this funny fellow his congratulations.

"We had better plows than this up in Iowa," Chester said shortly and continued down the row. But he was grinning to himself all the same, thinking that he could definitely count on making a living off these Wilsons if he just kept using his head.

When the dinner bell sounded and Chester came in to sit on the back step again, Lindy, still wearing her sack shift, brought him a plate with some dumplings and mashed potatoes and snap beans on it. From his kitchen chair Alistair watched Chester watching Lindy, and he knew he had another hold over Chester besides hunger if he wanted to use it. He smiled to himself and thought, Any man you got two holds over will work pretty cheap. At that point Alistair was still wavering on the question of keeping Chester, but later he found a third hold too, so that keeping him became irresistible. You might say Chester's vulnerability on so many points won him the place his determination and supposed cunning could never have gotten for him on our road.

The third hold depended on Chester feeling humiliated, which came about as a result of his asking after dinner, "Should I bring in the goat now?"

Alistair didn't want the rest of Chester's day wasted on a wild goose chase; he wanted him plowing. But when he began to say that Claude might do without his goat for one more afternoon, Chester got as uppity as he dared. "I've been gone a whole day already. Mr. Claude's going to wonder if I stole his goat. I don't want to be hunted down for a rustler."

Alistair picked the meat from his teeth, thinking. He could say that he'd sent one of his boys to deliver the goat to Claude so as not to disturb Chester's morning's work in the cornfield. But that would mean he'd have to make up the meal Claude owed Chester, in addition to giving him a supper for the afternoon's plowing Alistair was hoping to get out of him. That would be two meals but only one mealtime. The only way Alistair could think of to make up the extra reward was to offer Chester money, but of course that was out of the question. Then it crossed Alistair's mind that he could tell Chester straight from the shoulder they'd been funning him, but if he wanted a real job he was welcome to stay on a few days and see how he worked out. Alistair rejected that idea too, because he'd already talked to Chester enough to know it would kill him to find out he'd been made such a fool of. He'd probably take a swipe at Alistair's nose and stomp off the property. He might even linger in ditches and wait until he could set fire to some outbuilding at night.

Then Alistair got his brainstorm. He decided that he'd sent one of his sons to the back eighty that morning to check on the goat, and the boy had found the stake pulled up and the animal hiding in some tall weeds. He drew Chester over and told him this, and Chester looked like he believed it. So Alistair added, "Easiest way to find the goat now would be to keep chopping down those weeds till he doesn't have any more hiding places and you can corner him!" Alistair offered to let Chester use the scythe in the barn. Just enough shrewdness passed across Chester's brow at the mention of weed chopping to make Alistair add, "Naturally I'll be grateful for the work, so I'll be glad to feed you for as long as the job takes. And I'll send one of my boys down to tell Claude about the delay too." Chester's brow cleared and he found the scythe and walked off in the direction Alistair pointed.

Chester worked clearing that patch of ground for three days. If it had been covered with nothing but weeds, Alistair would have turned his cows loose to make some meals off them. But in fact it was a strip overgrown with brambles and small trees choking one another, useless for farming as it stood. No wonder Alistair had slipped a hatchet into Chester's hands along with the scythe.

Naturally Chester cut himself on the foot and bled badly one day, and he developed flaming blisters next to both thumbs so that he could barely hold his fork at supper. But he was eating regularly for the first time since he'd dropped from the freight ten days before. And when Alistair moseyed back the first evening to see how the work was coming, he had no complaints.

On Chester's first night, therefore, Alistair made Lindy understand that she would always carry the hired man's food out to the back step, rather than one of the children or the wife. So Chester, who'd been dreaming of goat and planning for tomorrow by the creek, was suddenly confronted by the neatly stitched hem of her feed sack as she bent down with his plate. Lindy never spoke, but her hands and her breath smelled like sweet milk. If Chester'd had the strength, he'd have stood up and tipped an imaginary hat.

Still, in those first days the goat was what kept Chester moving, even more than the food or the sight of the serving girl. Considering all the stories to come, I need to point out that Chester usually found himself in the grip of some obsession. Making it in Hickman had been his first one, and it had nearly starved him, though he couldn't have told you why he'd picked this particular town or what exactly he'd expected of it. Getting Claude's goat was a more specific goal, and with every bramble he hacked, Chester both hated and desired that animal more passionately.

The odd thing was that when Alistair asked Chester, the first evening at supper, "You seen that goat yet?" Chester replied, "I only caught a flash of him once or twice, heading deeper into the brush." That was a flash or two more than Alistair had expected. He forgot about all the jokes he'd been planning to make about Chester the next time he saw his brothers up the road and began to brood over the fact that every time Chester came in for a meal, he'd say something like, "Hacked my way within ten feet of that danged critter this morning, but then he bolted!"

What was Chester seeing out there that he mistook for goat? It occurred to Alistair one morning that nobody could be as stupid as Chester appeared. For one thing, he'd figured out how to hitch the plow. Was he biding his time, bellying up to the feed trough three times a day, deliberately keeping this goat fantasy alive in order to string his employer along, without ever being officially hired? The suspicion of such a trick made Alistair sniff sulphur.

So late on the third afternoon Alistair tramped back to take a more careful look. He caught sight of Chester hacking his way into a fenced-in corner high above the creek. With every swing of his tool he was muttering, "Gotcha now, gotcha now . . ." He looked like a perfect fool.

But Alistair was made so curious over Chester's frenzy that after a minute he couldn't help himself. He called out, "What you got there?"

Chester only pointed and resumed his frantic labor. Now Alistair found the excitement so contagious that in spite of his suspicions, he couldn't resist. He ran up and hissed, "You take one side and I'll take the other and we'll close in!" So the two men—one of whom had not believed until this minute that there was a goat within two miles—started inching toward the corner. Sure enough, Alistair heard a rustling in the thicket before him and then, as he and Chester edged nearer, some grass swayed and they heard a bestial grunt. "That's right, we gotcha now!" whispered Chester. Alistair was becoming alarmed.

And then it dashed out of the undergrowth and darted between them, zigzagging in its terror and eluding their outstretched hands. Chester sprang after it, downhill toward the creek. At the same time Alistair lunged too, tripping Chester and sending him spinning. He rolled thirty feet down the hill

and landed upon a heap of thorns he'd chopped, just short of
the water. When he tried to stand, he found that his left leg
wanted to buckle. But it wasn't until later that he noticed the
pain or worried that the injury might lead to a permanent
limp. For the moment he was too excited about nearly snagging the goat. "Did you see it run!" he crowed. "I'll get my
hands on that devil if it kills me!"

Alistair took a minute to find his voice before he asked, "Is
that what you've been hunting back here?"

Chester was still looking down the embankment toward
the little grove where the animal had disappeared. "That's
the closest I've got to him yet. Just wait!"

Alistair wasn't thinking of any strategy for handling
Chester now. If he'd taken time to piece out his alternatives,
he might not have risked the truth, but the whole event had
excited him so that he couldn't help blurting out, "That's no
goat! There's never been any goat! What you just saw run
past was an old sow that must've gotten loose and's been
living in the mud of the creek for who knows how long. The
last owners of this property were a shiftless bunch anyway—
I reckon they could've lost a sow into the bargain with everything else they lost." Then Alistair looked directly down the
hill at Chester and said, "Say, buddy, don't you know a goat
from a sow, you that plowed the whole state of Iowa?"

Chester sank back on his bed of thorns. There had never
been a goat! He had been hunting a pig!

The shock was so deep that the men entered a space where
those first two holds Alistair had over Chester—the food and
the girl—didn't count for anything any longer. Yet once he
heard his own words, Alistair realized how much he and his
brothers would lose if the fellow bolted out of fury at the
brothers for deceiving him, or at himself for not being able to
tell one farm animal from another. Consequently Alistair figured that if he wanted to keep Chester, he'd better go on
talking before the other could gather strength to move.

Sometimes you just have to throw your trust onto your own gift of gab and see if the words will come.

Alistair found the words sounding like bluster and he let them flow. "So you farmed when you were a boy, did you? I'll bet you milked the bulls and your roosters laid eggs! You know how much you're worth around here? About one meal a day and no wages. The only difference between you and my boy Rudy, who's six years old, is that your legs are longer and your belly's bigger—but as farmers you're the same."

Alistair's words felt so piercingly true that Chester couldn't even concentrate for the moment on how the four brothers had set him up with that billygoat, for he was beginning to see that the world didn't have a place for him anywhere, not even among the ignorant hayseeds. He'd just as well head back to town and lay his neck over the track and wait for the next freight to put him out of his misery.

Having reduced Chester's spirit, Alistair saw that it was time to show conditional mercy. So he opened his mouth again and the words came out: "Now, this big parcel of land was given me last winter, and it's more that I can handle. I'm late putting the seed in the ground already. So I'm going to take you on for a while, till something better comes along"— Chester looked up, startled at his undeserved good fortune— "but understand this: you don't know beans. So don't put on airs. You jump when I say jump!"

Chester would be allowed to eat at the table with the family, as a regular hired hand. He'd get the use of a small shed out by the well, where he could make up a bed. And when Alistair decided he was worth it, they'd have a conversation about wages. There were also a couple of other items about the arrangement that Alistair didn't mention. For one thing, Chester got to sit directly across from Lindy at the kitchen table, surrounded by Alistair and Sophie's brood of youngsters clamoring for helpings on either side. But to balance the pleasure of mealtimes, Alistair reminded Chester regularly that when he'd first showed up, he'd spent two days going from farm to farm in search of an animal that had never trod the earth and three days chopping down brambles because he couldn't tell one of God's creatures from another.

When the other Wilsons saw that the stranger was staying on at Alistair's, they asked him, "You found that goat yet?" or else they said, "Here's our old tin cans for Chester's pet to dine on!" The goat belonged to him now; my Uncle Claude had bestowed it on him. Even my grandpa thought the goat was a fair joke.

During the first couple of weeks Chester found no reply to these jibes, but his face turned into a turkey gobbler's and he stalked off, even if folks were about to sit down to a meal. When that happened, Alistair twisted his head at Lindy and she dished up a plate from the pots on the stove and took it down to his little cabin, where he sat fuming and about ready to head back to the depot to wait for a train. She never spoke, even when he lifted up his head and his chagrin turned into a stare of fascination and he muttered, "Thanks!" She smelled of the house always, of the fresh laundry or the savory kitchen, and as she turned away slowly—for she never hurried—Chester would look after her, marveling at the way her limbs moved inside that light shift she wore, fashioned from the feed sacks with the little purple flowers.

Chapter Two

Naturally Chester didn't realize at first that farm work wasn't the only reason why the Wilsons wanted him to remain among them, or why they went out of their way to josh him about the goat that was really a pig. To say what destiny they had in mind for him, I must explain about the family's stories.

Any time a neighbor stopped by one of the Wilson farms on his way into town to say howdy, or if a clerk at the Hickman feed and grain store looked like he had an extra minute to spare, a Wilson brother was likely to fix the other man with a sharp eye, clear his throat and start to chuckle, and a tale would commence. Generally the brothers told about some time when one of the Wilsons had performed an outrageous feat or delivered a stunning punch line, as if he was made of the same stuff as Paul Bunyan or Johnny Appleseed. And what I suspect is, the Wilsons' performances improved every time their deeds were told over. I imagine that they became stronger and slyer and harder to beat as their stories took on the forms I eventually heard.

Now, such stories as the Wilsons liked to tell didn't only involve themselves as heroes, of course; they also required somebody else as a dupe or victim for contrast.

But the gift of gab bedeviled them so that they could never rest with the stock of family legends they'd already accumulated. They were driven by a weird longing for more and more, as if they expected that in time life itself might finally take on the same form as all their stories. That's why they regarded Chester as such an unusual opportunity. His pursuit of Claude's goat had worked so beautifully, in fact, that they'd shared the sense of witnessing a miracle. For a few days life had come as close to working out like a tall tale as they could ever hope to see. Here was one time when they didn't even need to exaggerate the details: they could simply tell it like it had happened and crack their listeners up every time.

What's more, the Wilson brothers were fascinated by the way Chester's mind worked. He was so full of desire and hope and despair and useless longing—his brain was such a porridge of wit and anger and lust and boldness and futility—that he looked like a more delicious target than any they had ever encountered before.

Over the next few weeks they gave Chester plenty of chances to figure out what their love of storytelling might mean for an outsider. Every time Alistair worked alongside his new hired hand, or whenever the two of them sat in the cool of the evening together, one man whittling, one smoking, the Wilson stories would flow. Whenever three or four brothers pitched in to build a shed or restring a fence, or when they rode to Hickman together in the wagon with Chester slouched at the rear, one of them would cock an eye toward him and start up a tale.

Certain themes predominated—themes calculated to impress Chester with the lowness of his position in the Wilson scheme of things. While these stories were unfolding, he would often turn away his head and work his thin, worm-like lips as if his indignation couldn't be suppressed much longer—although the Wilson boys knew he had no choice but to hold his peace. Or he would whistle some tune to indicate that he wasn't listening at all. But the whistling would pause suddenly in mid-cadence, and he couldn't keep his cheeks from burning with exasperation. As a result, Chester in the act of pretending not to listen became a topic for yarns too—just as the tale about Chester hunting for his goat was widely repeated to a circle of neighbors, who knew those Wilsons could always tell a new one that was crazier than any they'd ever told before.

One of the classic family tales my great-uncles tortured Chester with that summer involves the time when Jethro, Tony, and Claude went to buy some hogs from a farmer near Saint Joe. Tony started it this way.

"This pig farmer, name of Lucash, had some shiftless fellows working for him who weren't much help, so he was glad to see all three of us show up to drive in the hogs with him. We acted like we were just as happy to see Lucash. We jumped out and clapped him on the shoulder and made a few jokes about the love life of pigs, till he was thoroughly tickled to be spending the morning with such agreeable folks. Then we followed him into the field and began walking up the herd, which numbered maybe eighty or a hundred.

"When we got the hogs up to the pen beside the barn, life became pretty lively for a while, with animals squealing and darting every which way. Now we were supposed to buy twenty. But as we walked among them, making our choices, we never left off talking to old Lucash. We asked him what he thought about an animal that looked lame, or we talked pork prices with him.

"Then we opened the chute onto the back of our truck, and Claude stood in front of it to let through the hogs we wanted. Meanwhile Jethro and I and Lucash started guiding the right ones forward. But during all that chasing and grunting, we never left off asking a question or telling a joke as we moved around the pen, to force a word or a laugh out of the pig farmer. We kept him on the far side of the herd from the truck, and when four or five hogs made a run to avoid the chute, somehow one of us always managed to stumble so that the bunch was directed toward Lucash, to make him jump.

"Finally the hogs were driven up till maybe thirteen, maybe fifteen were on the truck. Then I called over to Claude, 'How many we got?'

"Claude counted and said, 'Twelve!'

"'Good enough!' I shouted. 'Here, I'm sending you these two more.'

"On we went till maybe another half-dozen had run up the chute, then Claude counted again. 'Sixteen!' he called.

"While the counting went on, Jethro asked Lucash, 'What do you think about slops—do they turn the taste of the meat or not?' As the old man was answering, Jethro passed the latest word to him about the count: 'Just four or five more and we can quit.'

"'How many?' Lucash asked. But just then he had to dodge a pig, so he didn't hear the answer.

"We drove in another six and Claude shouted out, 'One more, make him a big one!' We let through one more and said that's it, so Lucash started to the house to get his receipt book. On the way in he called for one of his shiftless hands to let out the rest of the herd. Claude walked up beside him, talking all the time about what good-looking pigs they were, while we closed the back end of the truck. In the kitchen, Claude counted out the price on the table in fresh one-dollar bills. He did it wrong the first time—he put down a couple of dollars too many—and Lucash looked funny, so Claude asked, 'Did I make a mistake?'

"Lucash said, 'Might have.'

"Claude counted again, this time he did it right, and they both laughed over how easy it would've been for Lucash to pocket the extra money. Claude said, 'It's a good thing I always deal with honest folks, or I'd be bankrupt by now, because when I make a mistake, seems like it's always in the other guy's favor.'

"Lucash allowed that everybody these days was too poor to be a thief, so Claude didn't need to worry.

"Then my brother looked through the kitchen door and noticed we were starting the truck engine. He hurried out, calling good-bye over his shoulder. He jumped up on the running board as we passed through the gate, and I tugged him inside the cab. We were clean into the road before Claude had a chance to tell us the exact story. 'We took the old fool for twenty-seven pigs!'"

The last lines of that tale were invariable, no matter which of the brothers told it. "Old Lucash never missed them! Can you imagine—never counted his herd after the Wilsons had been among them! Heh heh heh!"

At this Chester would mutter to himself, "Well, what of it? Anybody that was scurvy enough could steal seven pigs." But he knew that in their eyes he was another Lucash, and they'd already gotten the better of him with a goat.

By late June the Wilsons' tales had begun to affect his enjoyment of his meals and his ability to sleep nights. Even though he was eating regularly for the first time in a couple of years, he found himself becoming as jittery as when he'd ridden the freights and feared a clubbing by a gang of railroad men every time the train slowed down. Any unusual event might cause him to balk at Alistair's instructions until he had been reassured that there was no deceit.

Even his view of Lindy across the dinner table was spoiled by the distraction. Sometimes at meals he would stare so hard at her that he forgot to take the fork from his lips, until the children at his elbows giggled and even the silent Lindy herself turned pink. But nothing ever seemed to click between them. Chester couldn't concentrate long enough to begin courting her in earnest so long as his indignation at my uncles' tales kept pulling his mind away.

His mood deteriorated further about cherry-picking time, when the Wilsons remembered a story showing how they'd mastered an uppity employee named Randall Sturgis. Jethro told it so that Chester couldn't miss the point.

"It was when Pappy died sixteen years ago that we each inherited our farms and could finally afford to marry. But the three of us younger boys lived on in the old house with Claude and his new bride for a couple of years, till our houses could be built on our own land. The only one who moved out right away was our sister, Jake's wife. She married as quick as she could and went to live on her own section, even though she had to start housekeeping in a lean-to. She didn't care to tarry among us brothers, because with her new husband she had a chance of getting her own way sometimes.

"Anyway, the building of our houses took longer than we'd expected, since we were all farming our land at the same time. From April to October we never had a free day. The first year we got the foundations in and the frames up, but then the skeletons just stood there waiting for the harvest to be gathered in. So we were glad when this fellow Sturgis walked up from Lathrop, carrying his tools in a canvas bag, and offered to finish them for us.

"He was the kind of carpenter that made every drawer fit perfect. Every door hung plumb. He took his greatest pride in his gingerbread. He designed it out of his own head, and he intended it for exactly one spot up at the gable or around the porch roof, and nowhere else. Even though Tony's and my houses are built to identical floor plans, you can see how the lines Sturgis wove gave them each a different cast. If it had been left to us, I don't know if we'd have bothered to design any gingerbread at all. Sometimes you just don't realize an advantage till it's shown to you.

"But like any child of the devil, Sturgis had his faults. He liked his rotgut and he drank it every night, so he was never ready to start work till nine or ten the next morning, and once he got over his hangover around noon, he set in whistling." (This detail was surely added because whistling was a nervous habit with Chester too.) "But we saw how fine the first house looked when he finished—it was Tony's, who's the oldest after Claude—so we held our tongues and paid his fee.

"Tony married the second of the Sledge sisters then, just like Claude had married the eldest of the four girls a couple of years before, and moved into his new place. Sturgis carried his tool satchel across the road to finish my house next. But the first day he made my jaw drop when he said his price was going up twenty dollars. Us Wilsons had made a mistake that played into his hands. We'd praised his work on Tony's place, so he knew how valuable he was to us. He and I faced off for a morning, but finally I agreed to pay what he asked.

"Well sir, once my house was finished and I married the third Sledge sister, the carpenter hauled his equipment down the road to Alistair's. Then came the news that his price was going up another fifteen dollars. Alistair told him, 'Wait till tomorrow,' so Sturgis sat on a pile of lumber all afternoon, smoking and sharpening his tools. At evening he went up to his room—he was still boarding at Claude's, because he was comfortable there—and uncorked a bottle, thinking he had us over a barrel.

"Now we knew he always dropped off from the whiskey about nine-thirty, so we waited till ten and then stole upstairs, bound his hands while he was conked out, and carried him to Claude's attic. There we tied him by the neck to a rafter, with his feet propped on a box. When he came to a little before dawn from the cold and the scratching under his chin, he let out some awful bellows, but nobody answered him till after breakfast. Then Claude poked his head through the attic door and asked, 'What's the matter, have the drunken blue devils got you?'

"Sturgis yelled to be let down. Claude asked, 'How much you charging my brother for finishing his house?' Sturgis roared out the price he'd set yesterday. Claude turned to leave, saying over his shoulder, 'Think about it.' At the sight of Claude's back Sturgis panicked and shouted another price, which was fifteen dollars lower, same as I'd paid him for mine. 'Come again?' Claude said, closing the door. Sturgis yelled another figure, which was the price he'd taken for the first house, the one that belonged to Tony. Claude held the door open a crack and smiled: 'Make it twenty lower still, to repay Jethro for that raise you stung him with, and you can come down to breakfast.' Sturgis glowered pretty fierce while he was being untied, but he didn't have much choice.

"You can see from the front of Alistair's house that Sturgis finished the gingerbread there faster than at the other places. Only one straight line of it over the front door. None at all on the gables or above the bay window. But all the drawers inside slide perfect, and the doors hang plumb. We left a coil of rope lying in the yard all the time he worked there, as a reminder of what we could do."

The first time Chester heard this story, he turned purple but said nothing. As each brother took his turn repeating it during the summer, though, the tale became embellished with comparisons directed at Alistair's new hired hand. Not only did the carpenter whistle now, but his nose slanted long and straight, he looked like a tall drink of water, he wore citified trousers. It was said that he pined after a wistful farm maid who—like Lindy—never spoke a word to her admirer. On the fourth telling Chester screamed, "Who the hell cares what you did to a stupid drunken carpenter? Nobody's going to tie me up like a dog! I never touch whiskey and I work plenty cheap already!"

But if he grew to hate those accounts of the brothers' triumphs, he was oppressed even more by a set of still older stories, which glorified the most intimidating Wilson of all, my Great-grandpa Harmon. This patriarch had homesteaded in the nineteenth century and lived to a great age, not dying until the 1920s. The brothers loved to talk about him. He was the man who had secured the family's prosperity for all time by snatching up the farmland he'd bequeathed to his four sons and his daughter. He was the man all my great-uncles dreamed of becoming, though Jethro and Tony were gracious enough to concede that only Claude had a chance of actually rivalling the old fellow. Alistair thought maybe a couple of the brothers had a chance, including himself.

The yarns about the original Wilson always started out with the ritual line, "Our pappy was so smart . . ." Claude would say, "He was so smart he wouldn't admit which field he'd been working in, you had to catch him coming back at nightfall if you wanted to know. He was so wicked cunning that when he came west to Missouri to homestead, he managed to trick the government land agent out of these six parcels we inherited, instead of settling for the single quarter he was entitled to. Why, he'd trick the new corn out of the ground!

"One time the wooden bridge that crossed the creek below the farmhouse where I live now collapsed under a neighbor's wagon full of grain. Tony here was just a tad then, but he saw the accident and ran in to tell Pa. So Pa went out and brought the farmer up to the kitchen, saying, 'Friend, you need a drop of corn liquor to collect yourself.'

"On the way in, Pa winked to a couple of us boys, who went down and hauled the wagon from the mud with the team and hid it beyond a hedge. When the farmer walked back a couple of hours later, he raised a cry that his wagon had been stolen. Jethro came along and said, 'Stolen! Why, there was a flash flood through here a half-hour ago that carried her off! You're lucky you weren't drowned!'

"The old farmer kept shouting, 'Stolen! Stolen!' but Jethro laughed and wandered off. The farmer tramped back to the house and confronted Pa, but Pa only said, 'If my son told you there was a flash flood, then there was one! My boys don't lie!' and slammed the door. The farmer paced up and down the road till dusk. Then he walked home. What else could he do, when he had no witnesses and the sheriff was sitting five miles away in town?

"That evening at supper we all noticed Pa was wearing a new brass pocket watch. While the farmer'd been drinking with him the watch had somehow changed hands. Pa kept a drawer full of watches he'd charmed off strangers over the years. Nobody knew how he managed it, because he always sat alone with them. He sent our ma and us out of the kitchen so he could talk man to man with his guest. Later you'd see him with the goods. His record was seven watches in a year."

As these bone-chilling tales worked inside him, Chester's indignation toward the family gradually took on broader implications. Years later he said to me, "It was when they told me all those stories about cheating and robbing and tying other folks up in knots that my blood really began to boil. I decided if they wanted to lump me with that pig farmer and the drunken carpenter and the neighbor who lost his watch, I wouldn't object. At least they were honest, God-fearing folks I was being cast with!"

While the brothers sat on Claude's porch telling their stories every Sunday afternoon now, Chester gazed at them across the lawn from his perch under a tree, just within earshot, and once he took up a stick and spelled in the dirt, "JUSTIS OR REVENGE?" At the crack of Alistair's laugh, coming at the climax of one of Claude's stories, the stick jumped, gouging deep into the last word.

My great-uncles may not have known exactly what was percolating inside Chester's brain, but as the harvest neared they were satisfied to see that his moods had altered. No longer obsequious or hopeful even at intervals, he lapsed into terrible black fits which the family found hilarious. Much as he sometimes pined after Lindy, there were moments when he couldn't even see her standing in the yard—he was that distracted. His reactions were so gratifying, in fact, that for several weeks the Wilsons didn't move to involve him in any new living stories like the one they'd already stung him with. They figured that anybody so inexperienced in the ways of farming, anybody who loses his temper so quickly (and lets you see he's lost it), anybody you've got three holds over— like hunger and shame and the nearness of a pretty girl— will always offer you plenty of chances. His agitation increased my uncles' confidence, and I can't really blame them. It's astonishing that after the episode with the goat they were never again able to shape a Chester-story entirely to their liking.

Much as they loved tormenting him with their tales, it was inevitable that they would finally grow restless and begin to look for some way to plunge him into a new action. Early in the season they had hugged themselves gleefully because Alistair had been inspired to put Lindy forward, so that Chester became infatuated with her. They had sensed that in the girl's apparent indifference lay the element that could ignite another living tale. But as the months passed, they still didn't see how this entanglement could resolve itself, since neither side was making any moves. Finally the delay began to annoy them. Yet they couldn't figure any way to speed up a romance, since what they knew best was only pigs and goats and dollar bills. So they had no choice on that front but to wait.

But it is characteristic of everything to come that when Chester's story with Lindy never seemed to start up, Alistair jumped the gun in another direction and then wished he hadn't. One afternoon early in the harvest, Chester became indignant when his boss said, "That grain'll carry itself to the barn about as fast as you're driving it in."

Chester shouted down from the wagon, "Damn your eyes!" and hopped off. He left the team standing in the middle of the field and wandered away to sulk in the cool of the barn. Now Alistair was used to Chester's temper, and normally he would have bided his time and waited for the apology that was sure to come. But today the goat story was on his mind, so he stepped to the barn door to see what he could provoke. He said, "Run down to Jethro's and ask to borrow his manure condenser, if you don't want to haul the grain."

Chester didn't know if he should be suspicious about this errand or not, but as a check he asked, "What's it look like, in case your brother isn't around?"

Alistair was so pleased with himself that his inventiveness ran away with him. He described the condenser as a metal apparatus resembling a medieval tower on wheels, about twenty feet high, with a metal weight of five tons held up by pulleys. When the weight was released, it fell down the length of the tower onto the manure, which was spread out at the bottom, and flattened it.

The story was too ridiculous for even Chester to credit. In fact, Alistair may have *wanted* Chester to disbelieve him this time, to realize that he was being sent on a futile mission as punishment for losing his temper, and that if he intended to keep his job, he had no choice but to ask at every house for the nonexistent contraption until the four brothers tired of their fun.

Anyway, Chester did complete the first move in the game. He asked at Jethro's as he was supposed to and was directed across the road to Tony's. But Jethro saw that Chester only feinted toward Tony's barn and then took off toward a pond, where he was probably planning to roll a couple of cigarettes before telling Alistair that the condenser couldn't be found.

Jethro's grin smoothed away and his eyes narrowed. He stepped over and hailed Tony and the two of them lit out toward that pond. Chester didn't have a chance. They tripped him up and pummeled him, then they swung him like a hammock ten feet into the water. They didn't wait to see him rise to the surface, though; they left him there to choose for himself whether he'd live or die. But as he crawled back to shore and tried his legs, Jethro called from a distance, "Next time you're sent to fetch a manure condenser, don't go home without it!"

This episode differed from the classic Wilson tales by its violence. It was one of the first signs that if properly roused, the brothers would put aside wit and calculation, and punish their opponent to within an inch of his life. But the next day Alistair fumed because his hired hand was so bruised that he couldn't work. The story left a sour taste in everybody's mouth, and the boys were sufficiently chastened that they laid off telling tales altogether for nearly a week.

At the same time, the beating confirmed to Chester that it was useless for him to lie low anymore. Alistair's third hold over him—the sense of shame before the superior knowledge of the brothers—had already begun to slip away, because he understood that regardless of how carefully he behaved, no Wilson would ever give him a break or regard him other than scornfully. And yet Chester still had no plans to leave Alistair's. For one thing, he was eating regularly. For another, the face of Lindy, serene above her mashed potatoes at dinner, haunted him intermittently. But maybe a more important reason now was that Chester couldn't subdue his outrage at all those Wilson stories that kept breaking out around him. "They drew me in, don't you see?" he said in later years, digging his stick deeper into the ground as he told over the story. "Got so I couldn't think about anything but Wilsons. Like they needed somebody to really hate them good, and I was the one God had put on earth to do it."

After his beating by the pond, therefore, Chester saw only one option: to launch a counteroffensive as boldly and cleverly as he could.

His first strategy, tentative and nonviolent, was guaranteed to backfire. None of the Wilsons subscribed to a newspaper in those days. There was a Hickman weekly, but it cost a nickel. The Saint Joe paper came out morning and evening, but it offered no rural delivery, and even if it had, the monthly charge would have seemed astronomical to a farmer. Claude owned a radio that sat in a great walnut cabinet, but a tube had burned out and he was waiting until he got the spare change to replace it. Consequently nobody ever heard much outside news. So it was rather surprising when, one afternoon as they were sharing a jar of water in the field, Chester asked what Alistair thought about Cordell Hull.

"Who's he?" asked Alistair.

Chester stepped back theatrically and demanded, "Why, don't you folks in the sticks know your secretaries?"

Alistair said, "I know Hull isn't agriculture. He might be commerce, or one of those that stick up for big business."

Chester snorted, "Why, if this country was left to the ignorant farmers, we'd all go down the drain!"

Alistair answered back, "You've living like a farmer now yourself, and you're eating better than you've ever eaten before, so you'd better thank your stars and shut up."

Chester said firmly, "He's the secretary of state, that's who he is. When I lived in Saint Louie I read the paper every day, and there he'd be, shaking hands with some foreign po-ten-tate. If you don't get a paper, how're you going to keep up?"

Alistair ordered him back to work, but Chester didn't mind. He had his opening. After that, every time he got a chance he harped on how uninformed country folks must be, and proposed to teach Alistair about the big world. Chester reacted differently now when Alistair or one of his brothers began a yarn about the Wilson family's exploits. He looked off calmly and waited until the narration wound to its end. Then, instead of stomping away mad, he treated their story as if it was innocent conversation and started in describing a related incident he'd picked up once from a Saint Louis newspaper. The Wilsons always found something to scoff at, or they shouted him down for wandering from the subject, but he could see that his offensive was having an effect, because the brothers didn't launch into so many tales now, and when they did spin one they were careful to cut it short. On the last sentence a brother would stand up and announce, "Let's get back to work, boys!" in order to keep Chester from replying.

In one way Chester felt the exhilaration of victory, for he had forced them to take defensive action to keep him in check. But his triumph was limited, since he could imagine no way to carry his thrust any further.

Until one Sunday afternoon after the Wilsons' usual communal dinner, the subject of cattle rustling came up. Not recent rustling, because in the thirties no animal was worth enough to bother stealing, but nineteenth-century rustling, as it had been recounted to the brothers by their father, my Great-grandpa Harmon. After they had spoken awhile, Chester responded with all he could remember reading about the Lindbergh kidnapping—about the baby, the ransom notes, the false leads, and Lindbergh sailing off the New Jersey coast in hopes of meeting the kidnapper, about the ransom money turning up in Brooklyn, about the trial, and the kidnapper's German accent, and the electric chair. The shadows lengthened, but none of the Wilsons tried to stop him, so Chester talked on. He seemed to be holding the brothers under a spell, so he had time to pace himself and work up his climaxes carefully. It was the first time he'd been allowed to show all he could do with a story, and he was proving that he could do almost as much as they.

After Chester'd told how the kidnapper had fried, none of the Wilsons said much, but they didn't reprimand him. During the next week, Alistair gazed at him thoughtfully once or twice, as if with a grudging new respect. The next Sunday after dinner, nobody else started talking, so Chester picked up where he'd left off. He began telling about the rash of kidnappings that afflicted Missouri businessmen in the thirties. Saint Louis, K.C., Joplin—no place was exempt from a band of four or five fellows holding a businessman until his company or his family paid up. "They make five thousand, sometimes thirty thousand. It's called the snatch racket," Chester chuckled, "because it's like snatching candy from a baby!"

After he'd told about a couple of the cases he remembered, the brothers spoke up for the first time that afternoon. "How could you snatch a man without anybody seeing you?" Tony asked. "What are your expenses?" said Jethro. "Where's the victim kept?" Claude threw in. And then the inquiries, which had seemed to arise from mere curiosity, began to turn sinister. "You know anybody personally who's been kidnapped over in Saint Louie, where you read all those newspapers after you gave up being a child farmer in Iowa?" "Or do you know anybody who's actually snatched a businessman?"

"Why, no!" Chester protested. "I never ran with crooks!"

They closed in pretty quickly after that. "To know so much about it," they said, "you must have been acquainted with somebody, or else you've been in the game yourself."

"Where'd you come from, anyway?" asked Claude. "Why'd you jump off the train in a little place like Hickman, when most tramps wouldn't look at it twice?"

"Searching for a hideout, I bet!" said Alistair.

"And what did you mean by saying that a good snatch takes four or five fellows to carry off?" Tony asked. "Were you meaning to propose—"

"Hell! I wasn't proposing anything!" he exclaimed. "These were just stories that I used to read every morning." His eyes rolled, searching the closed vault of the sky for a means of escape.

After that, every time he crossed paths with a Wilson he was sure to get sly questions about his past. Once Claude, grinning and taking his time, pushed the assault a step further. "You know you can't hide out forever. If they want you bad enough, they got ways of chasing you to the ends of the earth."

No denial fazed them. Chester became so furious with them for refusing to believe the plain honest truth about his past that he stamped his good leg and pounded his fist, but he could never turn their demonic inquiries aside. It seemed that his soul was a bloated white bladder and the four brothers were tossing it back and forth among themselves, all standing around an open well and laughing to see which one would throw short and lose it into the black water below.

He began to clam up after a week or so of this treatment. Finally they couldn't extract a word from him on any subject. My grandpa, who lived far down the road, saw what was happening plainly enough as he sat listening to the Wilsons after Sunday dinners. He wanted to sympathize, but Chester shrugged off everyone indiscriminately. Only when Alistair gave an order about the farm, he'd grunt and obey. His try at beating the brothers in storytelling had backfired. He needed an ally—not a peaceful-minded Christian like Jake Calder, but someone to plan with. He was convinced now that he could never whip the Wilson boys alone.

Chapter Three

Chester's big opening came because the family wasn't really as solid as it looked during that first summer. Shortly after his dunking in the pond, a couple of the Wilson women started moving as though feeling their ways in the dark, searching for a new configuration. And before you knew it, everything began to dance.

On the surface, the brothers' closeness was paralleled by an equal sisterhood among their wives. All the women shared the Sledge family's pale-moon faces and straight red hair, and the short mocking laugh. Kate, the eldest, had helped her ailing mother raise the younger ones amid the dirt and flies, and she loved her sisters with a fierce spark of possession. The younger three were accustomed to regard her, in return, almost as a mother, for she had taught them more about the handling of poultry and the way of ironing pleats than their real mother had.

The middle two sisters, Liza and Vera, formed a special bond reflected by their living across from one another in matching houses. Born only ten months apart, they seemed to have spent their childhoods standing side by side, opposite Kate, as she showed them how to plunge the butter churn. After marriage, they continued to ask their elder sister to decide a host of things for them, like which style of shoe to order from the Monkey Ward catalog, or what cure to use for melon worms.

Kate's manner wasn't dictatorial, any more than her husband would have laid down the law to his brothers. In the shadow of her mother she had learned to preside without openly expressing her authority. Sometimes she refused to give any opinion at all. But afterward, if Liza's or Vera's unaided decision turned out badly, her reproof took the form of a mighty silence which made the erring sister blush nose, ears, and elbows.

It's hard to say how Liza and Vera felt about surrendering to Kate in so many small matters. Did they bow to her from force of habit, or from honest admiration for her longer experience of life? Was a pleasing ritual gained by deferring decisions until Sunday, when Kate would weigh them in the lazy hours after dinner? Or wasn't there, too, a tinge of resentment at her power? The middle sisters were not sorry, as it turned out, to catch her that summer red-handed.

At first there seemed little chance that the eldest sister would stray. Her magnificent posture made her look solid as a rock. She had borne only two boys, Donny and Horace—now fifteen and thirteen—so her chores consumed less time than those of her sisters, who had to keep track of larger and younger families. Kate filled the idle hours by quilt making. She had counted twenty-three beds in the four Wilson houses, besides three more at her sister-in-law's house on the other side. Patching together a quilt for each one might have consumed a pleasant lifetime. But sitting in her sewing room with the cloth scraps spread around her during the long lonesome afternoons, humming a hymn tune or planning her supper menu, Kate would sometimes catch her hands lying idly in her lap, the needle threaded and waiting, and her mind—where had it gone? Then she would shake her head and say to herself, "Why, Kate Wilson, get ahold of your wits, girl!" No Wilson brother had ever awakened to such a moment, nor would he have understood what danger it signified.

The position of Sophie, the youngest sister by four years, was made precarious by the fact that all her life she had taken a more independent course than the middle two girls. By the time she'd grown out of diapers, all the chores in her parents' house had already been parceled out. Her sisters laughed over her little wide-moon freckled face and patched old dresses for her to wear, but they never treated her like an equal. Her role wasn't to fetch water or peel the beets, but to provide the rest of the Sledge family with a sort of living doll to marvel at. You couldn't call her spoiled, for Kate taught her to obey a direct command; but she did pout her lips often, and thought of herself as a person who might hope for indulgences. She made decisions not by drawing up a list of pros and cons like the other sisters, but quickly and by watching which way a lamb jumped in yonder field.

Originally the four Wilson boys had been intrigued by the fact that the Sledge girls formed a matching set just like themselves. They expected that their marriages, by providing them with identical experiences, would reinforce their brotherhood instead of splitting them apart. They had not forgotten when their pappy'd told them, "A single stick can be broken, but a bundle of sticks can't."

Courting the Sledge sisters, the Wilson boys never tried to act spontaneous. Claude, who went to the altar first, simply passed along to the next brother all his accidental or deliberate practices which had seemed to succeed with Kate. The second Wilson imitated his elder brother by rote, and then instructed the third brother how to court a Sledge in turn. So when Alistair at last stood beneath a harvest moon and presented his future wife, Sophie, with a princess made of two pink hollyhock flowers, the girl burst into laughter at his stiff gesture, since she'd been warned by her three elder sisters to expect it.

Still, the Wilson brothers pointed out in later years that they had reaped advantages from their strategy of treating the girls indentically. By comparing their observations, they had arrived at a science for discovering all they needed to know about their wives' minds. "Those sisters never whisper a secret that one of us doesn't shake out of them," Jethro would boast. "If Kate loses a carving knife, either I or Tony or Alistair'll report it to Claude by the weekend." What the brothers had sacrificed in individuality they made up for in absolute control.

Only, there had already been a few exceptions to that rule. The story went that when Alistair started courting Sophie, she knew full well that a betrothal agreement had already been signed by her father and old man Wilson seven years before. What's more, she felt the pressure of her sisters' expectations to follow where they had led. Alistair was broad-shouldered and washed his face and neck before riding over to visit her, so she had not hit upon any specific objections to him. But as the time for Alistair's official proposal drew near, some quirk in her soul raised its back. The night he offered her the hollyhocks along with his heart, she smiled to wonder what train of events she was setting in motion by batting her eyes and answering, "Why, I wasn't expecting anything like this at all! I'll have to think it over for a week or two."

Claude, red in the face and wondering if he smelled a swindle, pointed out to poor faint-hearted old Eleazer Sledge the next morning that the idea of Alistair marrying Sophie had been completely expected for most of a decade. Eleazer promised that his daughter was only shy, there'd be no hitch. And there wasn't. The wedding took place right on time a year later, when the carpenter, Randall Sturgis, finished Alistair's new farmhouse. But the other sisters did say among themselves, "How'd that bee get in the girl's bonnet?" Kate wondered if she'd been too lenient. Liza and Vera asked each other if the idea of needing a week to think over the proposal had ever crossed anybody else's mind? Of course it hadn't.

Being married to Alistair didn't give Sophie much time for caprice, though. The round of tasks enforced by the farm and by her six small children discouraged her from pining.

She knew that survival depended upon her just as much as on her husband. Still, the family continued to notice signs of a streak in her. If they came across her while she was doing her laundry, she might be weeping into the washtub for no reason at all. But the minute she saw a visitor, she'd brush away the tears with her wrist, laughing at herself for such foolishness and delighted to have some company. The next minute she'd be gabbling about a trip she'd taken to Saint Joe years ago with her Sunday school class. Consequently, when his brothers tried to advise Alistair about keeping her in line, they were forced to puzzle over the knotty problem that God hadn't made all the Sledge girls identical after all. If they could have predicted that anyone in the family would stray, they would have pointed to Sophie.

One sign of Sophie's desperation was that when Lindy came to work for her and Alistair the winter before Chester arrived, the mistress was unable to treat her young cousin naturally. One minute she thought of the girl as a shiftless poor relation: she was only the daughter of that no-good family who'd owned the eighty acres behind Alistair's place until they finally threw in the towel and packed up for California. Did they leave Lindy behind because they couldn't cram all their kids into the creaky old Chevy, and they felt more responsible for the little ones? Sophie wondered. Lindy behaved so coolly toward everyone that maybe she was the easiest possession to abandon when her parents had to choose between her and the camp stove. So sometimes Sophie became exasperated with the girl and shouted, "Get a move on with those dishes!" "Hang up that underwear straighter!" But the next minute she'd cry, "Poor thing, that pail's too heavy for you!" Lindy's bones were small, her cheeks thin. She'd gotten out of the habit of eating before she came to live with her cousins, so on hot days she merely pushed the food around on her plate while everybody else was sweating and chomping away. Her pale complexion resembled a china doll's—appealing to Chester, who'd known only roughness before, but it was a faint and sickly beauty. Sometimes Sophie's heart melted so she thought she ought to take a week off and just nurse the poor girl with broths and special cakes and pies.

Despite her pathetic looks, though, Lindy's silence kept her from engaging Sophie fully. There's only so much sympathy you can feel for a statue, after all. That's why, when Alistair hired Chester, the wife's attention was still partly at large, and she began to look over the new hand to discover what possibilities he might offer. The result was that one Saturday at dinner, Alistair said to Chester, "The wife wants you to go along to church tomorrow." Alistair spoke indifferently, as though referring to a barnyard chore. But the idea did infringe on Chester's morning off, which he usually spent in his cabin smoking and mending his clothes, or else walking a creek bank and drawing his own religious conclusions from crawdads and mud.

So Chester threw down his fork and asked in a high, dramatic voice, "I just wonder if there's still freedom of religion in this country? I'd just like to know if I can't pray by myself instead of traveling into town?"

Alistair continued to eat, abandoning the affair to his wife, who pointed out shrilly, "Every other family who owns a hired hand"—"owned" was her word: Missouri had been a Border State—"carries him to church in the back of their wagon except us. It's a disgrace to let folks think our man's not even respectable enough to be seen."

Chester grumbled all afternoon, but the next morning he dressed in one of Alistair's clean work shirts that Sophie had altered for his narrow chest, and climbed into the back of the wagon with the children. He was still licking his wounds from the beating at the pond, and had no strength to disobey.

His only consolation on the journey into town was watching Lindy's freshly washed hair wave around her pink ears in the wind.

The hired hands who sat in a sullen, seedy bunch at the back of the nave did not appear devout. The most you could say was that they kept quiet during prayers and stood whenever the preacher lifted his arms as a signal for the hymns. Most of them looked to be little older than boys. Chester glanced up and down the row to determine if he might smoke, then put his tobacco and rolling papers back in his pocket.

He expected the hour to pass tediously, and certainly it might have, except that something struck him funny about the preacher, whose name was Selkirk. Hadn't he seen that fellow driving past Alistair's farm in a dusty old Model A with one of the headlights batted cockeyed? And wasn't he about the greasiest bear of a fellow you ever saw, with huge mangy tufts of hair sprouting from all the visible areas of his flesh, and wide nostrils that expanded like he was sniffing sulphur when he spoke? And how could you forget the trombone slide of his voice, which might start a sentence up in heaven, but descended by degrees into pitch-black hell as he guessed at your nastiest sins and flashed you his knowing leer? This preacher's eyes glowered out of a thicket of whiskers and brows, roaming his congregation for the wickedest sinner in the room, stopping often to glare at a particular young lady down front, frilly and distracted, until he had reduced her to a rainbow of blushes. He raked the row of hired hands with his enraged stares until even the most irreverent drifter straightened his back and dropped his head toward his lap. Selkirk knew sin—anybody could see that—and he knew how to fashion brimstone with his lips. Chester had to concede that in his line, he was a professional you wouldn't want to mess with. The odd thing was that, during the singing right after the sermon, when the preacher was mopping the sweat from his brow and glancing about the room, he kept returning to meet Chester's eyes, as though trying to place him, or, since this preacher seemed so deep, perhaps he was measuring Chester to see what kind of newcomer he was and what work he was fit for.

After the service Selkirk loomed at the door, solemnly shaking hands with his parishioners. Chester's curiosity had been aroused by now, so he watched closely when he saw Sophie eagerly pushing her brood of children forward among the crowd until they reached the holy man. She made each little one touch the hirsute fist. After that the mother, red-faced from bustling, continued to block the other folks wait-ing to file past. Shyly she bowed her head as Selkirk spoke in a low tone. "You look like God's own sunshine this morning, Sister Wilson!" Meanwhile Alistair hung back, apparently indifferent to the scene at the door, trading quiet jokes with some men.

The hired hands waited by their pew until everyone else had passed outside. Then as they followed the crowd, the preacher suddenly vanished through a side door to avoid dirtying his hands with them. But as he closed it, he turned his head briefly to measure Chester's face once more. Chester could not decide if the little bob of his head was a nod, or if it was only caused by the rise and fall of his step through the doorway.

Outside, Sophie had recovered her composure and acted as if she was thoroughly gratified by Chester's first visit to church. Several ladies asked each other loudly who he be-longed to, and her sisters smirked to congratulate her for bringing him into line. But except for the preacher's peculiar stares and the prickle of wonder he felt as he overheard Sel-kirk's greeting to Sophie, Chester received no immediate re-wards from his morning of worship. When he attempted to make friends with the other hired hands standing at the edge of the churchyard, they acted so tongue-tied and silly that he became disgusted with them. None had the nerve to laugh at his sarcasm about farmers who made their employees waste a fine morning like this indoors among the hypocrites.

He climbed into the wagon discouraged. On the way back to Claude's house, where all the Wilson families were taking Sunday dinner together as usual, Lindy again sat up front behind the driver's seat, holding two of Sophie's little girls loosely around the waist. Chester kept far to the rear and waited morosely for her face to turn toward him. It never did.

Still, that first glimpse of Selkirk in his pulpit was a necessary preparation for beholding the scene that occurred the following Tuesday afternoon. Alistair and Chester were bringing in a wagon filled with hay from one of the fields bordering the road. At a distance of a few hundred feet they could see Sophie sitting among her children in the yard. She was coring apples for pies. Lindy must have been in the kitchen. Suddenly a rolling cloud of dust on the road announced a car, which slowly turned into Alistair's driveway. It was old and black, and one headlamp stem bent downward as though suffering a perpetual humiliation. The car hulked to a stop near the house, and as the puff of dust caught up and dissipated, a short, barrel-shaped man got out.

Just as Chester recognized the preacher, Alistair shook the reins and yelled, "Giddap!" The team, burdened by their load, could not hasten much. Alistair grew incensed by their pace and suddenly threw the reins to Chester. He jumped down with a growl and began running across the field toward the house. Chester slowed the team to a walk and watched as Alistair dashed onto the lawn and grabbed the preacher's shoulder. Selkirk had been standing before Sophie, apparently passing the time of day, but now he was wheeled around to face Alistair and given the bum's rush back to his car. Sophie stood up and her pan of apples fell to the ground. Alistair snatched the preacher's hat from the grass and threw it into the front seat after him. The car started up and backed crazily toward the road. Sophie was screaming at her husband. None of the words quite reached Chester's ears, and he couldn't believe his eyes.

Late that summer Claude's older son Donny started walking the mile and a half to Alistair's place most evenings after supper. At first it wasn't clear what he wanted. Alistair and Chester would be sitting in the yard, with the six kids playing around their father. Sophie and Lindy banged away in the kitchen, cleaning up. Donny said "Hi!" very shyly and stretched out by the men on the lawn. He spoke softly about the weather, which was invariably muggy, or the progress of the harvest at his end of the road. Chester was saying nothing to anybody those days, and Alistair divided his time between his children and the visitor. Donny soon exhausted his short string of topics and fell silent, picking at the grass. His beard had started but he hadn't yet begun to smoke. Finally the kitchen noises subsided. As twilight settled over the broad fields and the fireflies began to wink, the women came out to sit on the step and fan themselves.

Donny spoke politely to his Aunt Sophie and then said something more elaborate to Lindy. At first she only answered "Hi!" but after a few visits Donny rose from the ground one evening when she appeared and walked over to sit near her. He tried a few gambits which she answered almost inaudibly, "Yes, I guess" or "I don't know." Sophie had been gazing off toward the road, as though the two young folks didn't concern her, but after ten minutes she told Lindy, "Time to wash the children for bed!"

Chester watched Donny's face fall as Lindy went over to pick up the baby wallowing at Alistair's side. After the women said good night, Donny quickly rose and left. A few minutes later Sophie reappeared and spoke to her husband. "I can't think where Kate's wits are, letting her boy come calling on the girl like that. We don't want her shiftless kind marrying into the family."

Alistair shrugged. "She's living amongst us already. Besides, there's too many Wilson kids now to get them all wives the same quality as us four got. If Claude doesn't want Donny chasing after Lindy, he'll speak to him pretty soon."

But Claude didn't interfere, and Kate's thoughts seemed to wander elsewhere when Sophie confronted her on the matter, so four or five nights a week Donny appeared, the same shy smile, the same ill-placed adolescent giggles, the same mooncalf look when Sophie sent Lindy inside earlier and earlier with the children.

Donny didn't always depart immediately, though. Finally Alistair would say good night to his nephew and go inside too, leaving only Chester sitting in the near-darkness by his cabin, his cigarette smoldering orange as he watched the boy, who looked up at the second-story windows of the big house, dreaming his dreams. If he was waiting for Lindy to peer down and wave or blow a kiss, Chester saw that she never did.

Before Donny started coming to admire Lindy, Chester had almost resigned himself to her indifference. After all, she was family and he wasn't, and she had observed him being slighted and scorned. Besides, he was twelve or fifteen years older and his teeth were rotting, so he admitted to himself that maybe a creature like her was best enjoyed from afar. But when Donny's intentions became plain, Chester could scarcely control himself. The spectacle of the boy waiting beneath her window in the dusk drove him to fury. If she had ever appeared then, Chester might've done something he'd regret, like hurling a handful of chicken droppings at the back of his rival's neck. When the girl never showed her face, though, and Donny shuffled off forlornly every night, Chester's jealousy began to cool. He drew comfort from Lindy's refusal to encourage a swain more her own age.

If she was indifferent toward everyone, then all could live in peace.

In this tolerant frame of mind, Chester at last approached the boy as he sighed alone into the hot night air. But Chester's motives weren't wholly innocent, at that. He was on the look-out for allies now, as I've said, expecting a long struggle against the Wilsons. Realistically, he couldn't suppose that Donny would assist him in the out-and-out battles to come. But if Chester was able to shape the boy's attitudes, then Donny's friendship might open the way for launching some sneak attacks on the rest of the family.

Donny was surprised when Chester called, "Hey, boy!" since he had thought he was alone beneath Lindy's window in the darkness. But he wasn't ungracious until Chester asked, chuckling, "You think she's up there stretched out on her mattress now? What must she look like, with her bare arms spread and her mouth open, just breathing in and out?"

As Donny's face turned from surprise to revulsion, Chester smilingly pursued his vision. He was ready to patronize the youth, to educate him about the painted ladies of Saint Louis and the casual encounters he had stumbled into during his months riding the rails. He knew a few raucous jokes too, one of which employed three fingers of the human hand for demonstration.

Donny had seen newborn calves licked clean by their mothers' tongues; he had held just-hatched yellow chicks in his hand. In the same spirit he pined after Lindy with all the tender force of his young heart. He was shocked by the common lust in this hired hand's imagination. Before Chester could even tell a second joke, Donny shouted, "What're you saying, you filthy man!" and lit out toward home, as though wind and speed might clear his ears of that filth.

Hearing the shout in the yard below, Alistair, who was pulling off his overalls in the dark, smiled to himself. Succeeding evenings confirmed his hopes. Donny never returned

Chester's oily greetings now. The mooncalf ignored the hired hand and kept away from him. There was unmistakable disgust on the youth's face at the thought that such a low creature, whose mind was a sty, could eat at the same table "she" ate at, or sit near her in the yard every night, smoking his infernal cigarettes and littering the territory with his grublike butts.

Next time they were alone, Alistair spoke to Claude about Donny's hatred of Chester. Claude laughed. "She'll keep the two of them biting and kicking, all right!"

Neither man much cared about Donny. They assumed he was driven by simple barnyard jealousy and lust. But he was too young to marry yet, so the main thought that flashed between father and uncle was that an antagonism between Lindy's suitors might be the catalyst they'd been waiting for. Maybe without their having to engineer it, the great tale that Chester had in him was finally going to be acted out before their eyes.

As the harvest passed from hay to corn, Alistair and Claude often drew apart to talk alone. Chester noticed that they had become a distinct group among the brothers, the oldest and the youngest. Often now when Donny walked down to sit beside Lindy of an evening, his father would accompany him and wait by the mailbox until Alistair put his babes aside and strode out for a conference.

Even from a distance Chester could tell that the brothers' words were not spoken in the jovial rhythm of storytelling. He could hear no laughter floating on the night air. After Claude and Donny left, Sophie never asked her husband what Claude had wanted. Clearly the men had been exchanging bitter intelligence, and Alistair would not have stood questioning by anyone. He sat with his own thoughts then, not heeding the noise of his wife going inside to bed.

Throughout those puzzling weeks Chester caught glimpses

of the goggle-eyed Model A creeping up and down the road inside its cloud of dust, as though moving through the landscape under military camouflage. It seldom stopped anywhere, but it advanced so slowly that it seemed at every minute about to turn into one of the Wilson driveways. The preacher appeared to scan the fields for sight of harvesters, but once he located Alistair and Chester he would drive past, make a U-turn at the far intersection, and then retreat toward the other three Wilsons' farms.

Particles of dirt and straw hung thick in the air as Alistair and Chester filled the wagon time after time. They wore wet red bandanas over their noses like bandits for protection, but above Alistair's bandana his gray eyes restlessly scanned the road, waiting for the Model A to reappear so that he could curse it.

Since the back eighty had been planted late, it would be harvested late. But Chester began to wonder why Alistair kept putting it off, finding odd jobs for them around the barn instead, even though the fields had finally ripened. It looked as if he was afraid to work so far away, as if he wanted to keep in sight of the road and the house.

Meanwhile Chester was still expected to join in the family's weekly trip to church. But he didn't grumble now. He was eager to go, and studied Selkirk's every expression up in the pulpit, straining to read his mind. The sermons still flamed hellfire and the preacher's satanic eyes still scoured his congregation mercilessly. But Chester was satisfied to find, looking closely, that Selkirk kept his eyes open during the prayers, when all other heads bowed low. And one Sunday as Selkirk walked away from the church door after shaking hands with his respectable parishioners, in order to avoid that mongrel bunch of hired hands, he looked straight at Chester and suddenly winked. "How-do!" he said distinctly, and then vanished through the side door before Chester could recover from his surprise.

At last Alistair couldn't postpone working in the back eighty any longer. But during the middle of the afternoons he invented some task that required him to remain around the barnyard while Chester was sent off to bring in one more wagonload by himself. Of course Chester was new to harvesting, so his trips took too long and he left much of the crop scattered in the field. Finally, as an experiment, Alistair drove the wagon back for the final load himself, leaving Chester at the barn to shovel grain. Chester had received no special instructions, but clearly his presence was supposed to act as some sort of deterrent. He was not surprised when, after half an hour, he saw the invading cloud of dust roll down the road. It paused next to Alistair's mailbox for a long minute and then disgorged the black Model A into the drive.

Chester leaned into a shadow and watched as Selkirk first stood beside the car and sniffed the air, then walked quickly to the kitchen door and knocked. Sophie met him, looking flustered and plumping her hair with both hands. They disappeared inside without a word. Chester took up his shovel again, but he worked with his face toward the house. After twenty minutes the preacher reappeared in the doorway alone, threw a good-bye into the kitchen, and hurried toward his car. This time Chester took the dare of stepping from the barn door into the sunlight. When Selkirk saw him he nearly jumped with fright, but, finding it was the hired man and not the master, he converted the jump into an accidental-on-purpose stumble and extended his hand, walking down to where Chester stood.

"O heavenly sunshine!" the preacher called for greeting. "Is Brother Wilson around?"

"Working the back eighty."

At that the preacher wiped his face and decided to talk a spell. He began with the usual litany of crops and prices, throwing in a fractured biblical saying now and then, while Chester kept up his end as well as he could. All the time Selkirk was pressing, though, at the name of Wilson to see what fire he might raise in Chester's tongue. He asked, "Is Brother Alistair Wilson's harvest going as fast as Brother Claude Wilson's?" He said, "I hear Brother Tony Wilson's and Brother Jethro Wilson's crops are already gathered in like saints to Abraham's bosom."

When Chester remarked, "This harvest can burn in hell as far as I'm concerned!" Selkirk pushed even harder, asking if Chester didn't agree that the name "Wilson" had a fine round sound. "It fills the mouth like hymn singing. It makes you think of the majestic sweetness of the Lord's bounty."

Chester replied, a bit provoked and wondering at the same time if he had guessed Selkirk's secret, "The only Wilsons I got any interest in wear skirts."

The preacher paused, and Chester feared he might be dressing up a sermon on carnal temptations. But it turned out to be a pause of thoughtful appreciation. Selkirk extended his arms in a pulpit gesture and began, "We can see all around us the beauty of God's hand. He gilds the grasses in harvest, He ripens the fruit of tree and vine. Is it any wonder He adorns man's home with His most glorious work, the face of Woman?" A sly shadow passed over his face as he added, "The face and the body!"

Chester's eyes bugged a little; then he grinned. Selkirk nodded and took them one step further. "Yes indeedy, they are divine! Why, everything else the Lord made is just to remind us of them. Like that mowed field over yonder, the way the yellow stipple sticks up all over it—same as the tiny hairs on a woman's belly in God's early morning light."

Now Chester could not keep back his laugh of recognition and release. His bowels twitched to think of such ideas being expressed through the preacher's holy words. "Truly, truly, preacher, everything does make me think of women! It must be the Lord's will!"

Selkirk must have experienced an irresistible pleasure too

at the declaration he had allowed himself, and he tingled with delight at the fellowship he was suddenly discovering with this kindred soul. "Truly, truly, praise God! We got nothing to do but enjoy them!"

Chester could have clutched himself for happiness. After that, they unbent to one another in a rush. Within five minutes Chester had gotten down to the crude jokes he had wanted to tell Donny. Selkirk never quite laughed, he held his eyes to the ground, but his ears turned bright red and his fingers kept pulling at the knots of hair on his wrists, as if the animal in him couldn't keep still for joy to hear another fellow say such things.

Finally Chester mentioned that he'd seen the preacher's car snooping around lately. Selkirk wanted to extract some information too. "Seems like Brother Alistair doesn't care for my prayer sessions, does he?"

"What prayer sessions are those?" Chester asked.

"When they're alone, Sister Sophie and Sister Kate invite me in to pray with them. Of course I'd rather kneel beside Sister Sophie, because she's prettier, though Sister Kate's easier to find by herself. It's unchristian how the husbands seem to oppose me, when their wives are so anxious for it."

Chester paused a minute, measuring the preacher's tone; then he made a crude remark about how the women must look on their knees with their hands clasped. Again the preacher didn't laugh, but he confirmed Chester's innuendo by the way he snorted and rubbed the back of his hairy hand across his nose. Somehow the thought of Sophie together with Selkirk stirred Chester's imagination powerfully. It wasn't necessary for either man to explain why he wanted the Wilson women debauched, and why they were both especially glad Selkirk might be the one to do it. The preacher offered only a brief defense of his lust. "Adultery's the seventh commandment. There's lots of sins worse than number seven." After that, their conversation quickly turned to the ways of cuckolding.

Selkirk swore that he'd never yet had the chance to carry a prayer session to its climax. A child was always bawling or a husband showed up from the barn just when the coast had looked clear. "Why, even today, I wondered if I heard your shovel scraping out here, so I figured I'd better say 'Amen!' and get to the door." If only he could reassure one of the wives that they wouldn't be interrupted for an hour . . .

"I'll work on it," Chester told him fervently. "We'll get us a plan. But meantime you'd better lay low during daylight, because old man Wilson's getting fidgety. I don't know what he'd do if he caught us together."

That evening Alistair asked if Chester'd seen anything while he'd been left alone at the barn. But when Chester said no, Alistair let him alone and fell to brooding. He was too preoccupied with his own suspicions to notice that Chester, instead of lounging among the shadows in the yard as usual, wandered off along the creek that crossed the road below the house. He found the Model A parked near the bridge in a patch of tall weeds.

The two plotters agreed they had to act fast. Alistair would be at work on the back eighty only two days more. Chester's role was to guarantee that he'd keep his employer away from the house the next afternoon come hell or high water. Selkirk was confident he could raise his Ebenezer and do the rest.

Tony and Jethro loved to tell the climax of this story. "While they were out in the field the next day, old Chester and Alistair got into half a dozen arguments. Chester did everything he could to get his boss's goat. He stopped work every half hour to tie his shoes, or he stood for a whole minute with the water jar to his lips, not drinking, but like he was feeling too delicate to go on loading the wagon.

"Then every time Alistair said, 'Let's get a move on,'

Chester started in defending himself, and before long he was whining about all sorts of complaints that he'd been nursing since the beginning of summer. He was aiming for a knockdown-drag-out shouting match. Only Alistair couldn't keep his mind entirely on Chester those days, and besides, Chester wasn't making too much sense. Finally Alistair just told him to bring in the wagon by himself if he ever got it full and started off on foot toward the house, to check up on things. Quick as he could, Chester called out, 'Wait!' My brother turned his head, still walking away. At that point Chester was so desperate he went stupid. He shouted, 'The team's got loose!' Alistair looked at the horses that were standing in harness under some shade trees by the fence and just shook his head. Then he went on toward the house. So there was nothing Chester could do but creep along behind and watch the disaster.

"When Alistair got to the back of the barn and peeked around it, he was surprised to see Claude standing next to the Model A that was parked in the drive. It turned out Donny had walked over to Alistair's that afternoon, probably pretending to borrow a tool or something, but really to catch another sight of Lindy. He'd seen the preacher's car there and had run home to tell his dad. I doubt that Donny really understood what was going on, but at least he'd picked up that us Wilsons didn't like the preacher nosing around on our road, so he figured this looked suspicious—especially when nobody answered his knock at the kitchen door.

"Nobody answered the knock because when the preacher'd showed up, Sophie'd sent Lindy down to the creek with the babes for a picnic. She'd thrown a heap of jam and sugar cookies into a sack and told them to take their time. Meanwhile Claude showed up—without Donny—but he did think to bring along a couple of pitchforks." Here the brother who was telling the tale would nod decisively.

"Alistair came up just then and took one of the forks without more than a couple of words, and Claude went around to guard the front door while Alistair slipped into the kitchen. Then a roar came from inside the house, and a crash of glass from around in front. In another second here came Selkirk running across the lawn, chased by two men armed with the forks. Twice they poked him in the backside and he let out tremendous yelps that sounded like a wounded bear. 'Holy holy holy! O the trump of Judah! You saints and sinners better beware!' While he was running he tussled with his pants to fasten them. Finally my brothers dropped back and Selkirk ran up the road toward town. Left his Model A beneath the tree. My brothers waved their forks after him in the air. Then Claude went home to ask his Kate if she wanted to hear a story about what happens to a wife that lets a preacher in to pray with her, and Alistair went back inside his own house, still carrying the pitchfork, to settle with Sophie.

"Yes, sir, old Chester must have gotten his eyes plenty full before he slunk back to the field alone!"

For the next couple of weeks the harsh, conquering laughter of the brothers resounded up and down the road. Jethro and Tony told and retold the story of the joint attack, the preacher's howling departure, and the scene the next day when he rode a borrowed horse out to Alistair's place to beg his car back. Alistair was sitting on the running board waiting for him, and he turned over the preacher's hat and coat as well as the Model A. He had doused them in kerosene, possibly to carry out the infernal theme of the pitchforks. Just button up and light a match . . .

But when either of those brothers told the story, he always insisted, "Sure, he never had time to lay a hand on her!"

At Sunday services now the Wilsons sat with their heads high and their eyes wide open, staring Selkirk down. Smiles passed among them which they made no effort to control. If the preacher lost his place during Scripture readings, they nudged one another and chuckled noisily. His sermons, formerly thunderous, were now delivered in a sheepish mumble, though sin and its wages remained his only theme; he appeared to have no conception of mercy. And why should he have? The Wilson brothers might have presented their story to the church's governing board and got the preacher dismissed immediately, but they preferred to exact their punishment slowly and exquisitely, by innuendo and scorn.

Chester was dragged to church every week as usual and sat morosely in the back pew, counting the minutes until he could roll a cigarette. He and Selkirk avoided each other's eyes now, even though Chester would have liked to assure him that he'd done all he could to carry out the plan, and besides, he wanted to ask how far the prayer session had progressed before the interruption. But he couldn't risk a communication, for Alistair would be sure to notice and connect him decisively with the preacher's offense.

My grandfather was no storyteller in the Wilson mold, but for that reason he was perhaps a better observer than they. On those early autumn Sundays when Grandpa watched Chester skulking at the edge of the family circle, he detected that the Wilson boys seemed to hold the hired man under some terrible suspicion. They acted as if they had beaten him too when they had chased Selkirk away from their wives, and were only lacking some final bit of proof that would justify stringing him up by his toes. At the height of their boasting they turned to gloat directly at him, forcing him to bow his blushing face. Grandpa didn't know how right their suspicions were, though; he supposed they were just bullying Chester according to their nature, and there was nothing he could do to stop that.

If his Sundays became more miserable after Selkirk's defeat, Chester's workaday life also took a turn for the worse. After Alistair disciplined Sophie, she did not emerge from the house for many days, nor was Chester allowed inside it. His meals were brought down to his cabin, usually by a child young enough to spill several morsels on the way.

Lindy darted in and out now, moving faster than she ever had before, busy with the household chores as well as the poultry and the squirming babes. Meanwhile Alistair made a point of spending his evenings with his brothers at one of their houses down the road, forsaking his wife's company. Consequently Chester found himself passing nearly all his leisure hours by himself now, as if he was nothing more than a piece of farm equipment stored in a shed at night.

It wasn't lost on him that his second act of rebellion, and the first one he'd planned carefully with an ally, had failed utterly. He thought too about the fact that for the second time in a season, two brothers had ganged up on an outsider and hurt him cruelly. Besides heaven knows what Alistair had done to Sophie with the fork handle that made her not want to show her face. How bloody might their revenge be on the next occasion, especially if all four acted at once? So Chester sprawled alone in the night air, down by the well or underneath a tree, wondering if he should cut bait and get out while a month of fair weather was left for riding the freights. Maybe what stopped him was that once or twice during his meditations, as he stared up bitterly at the farm-house, he caught the unforgettable sight of his mistress's pained raccoon eyes through the kitchen window, glowing like darkest hell as they sought the path where Selkirk had run, high-stepping it in fear of his life.

Chapter Four

All the Wilsons made money off their harvests that fall for the first time in four years. The ponds the government had urged farmers to dig finally started to fill, and the streams ran up to their banks again before winter. Prayers were spoken—that is, Selkirk was obliged to offer thanksgiving steadily for three months, until everybody had gotten used to the idea that they might survive and he could safely drop the subject. Claude talked about buying back the De-Soto he'd sold to a dealer in '34; it was still sitting on the lot in town, the paint job not much worse for the weather.

Lots of things about that autumn felt right again—lots of the fundamental things. After their haylofts were filled and the farmers had sold part of their grain at the elevator, they could settle into a slower pace and sniff the air. They could pause to watch the sky pile up with clouds, and they remembered those persimmons they'd spotted in the woods that the frost would ripen soon. If they'd planted a sugar maple, they found themselves kicking through piles of fingered plates as big as your hand, and they couldn't help lifting their knees higher with every step at the illusion of life and power created by that crunching sound.

Autumn was also the time when a farmer began to formulate projects, since he was no longer a slave to his crops. At last he could repair the smashed boards on his wagon, or slaughter a couple of animals he didn't want to carry through the winter. That fall after Selkirk had been chased off Alistair's property, Jethro and Tony both decided to repaper a couple of rooms where their wives had been complaining about grease spots on the walls. They sent Liza and Vera into town one morning with a few dollar bills and told them to pick out the loudest patterns they could find. Alistair and Claude didn't happen to get any ideas about treating Sophie and Kate like that, but they did find time to socialize more away from home, at auctions or else hanging around the Hickman feed and grain on Saturdays. Since Sophie still never showed her face, even at church, and Kate often felt under the weather, their husbands always drove out on these trips with one of their sons or else alone.

In fact, Sophie's bruises didn't clear up for weeks, and she was still hobbling a bit as late as Thanksgiving. That left Chester in the cold at meals and during the long evenings, huddled down at his cabin stoking his little wood stove. Occasionally after one of the children had taken away his supper plate and cup, Alistair would stop at the cabin on his way to the council of brothers that had begun meeting every evening down at Tony's or Jethro's. But when Alistair poked his head in, he was all business. He gave instructions about tomorrow's work, or else he introduced the next stage in their long negotiations about whether Chester would be kept on over the winter.

On Alistair's side the discussion was mostly bluster. "I suppose you want to stay and eat my meat while there's no income . . ."

In return, Chester complained, "This cabin isn't fit for the cold and besides, the cooking around here's sure fallen off since Lindy took over in the kitchen." Not that he wanted to get the girl in trouble, but he couldn't control his tongue when he felt insecure.

Both men were nervous about the outcome of these conversations, since Alistair had his complicated reasons for wanting Chester to stay on—without pay—while Chester, though he'd considered leaving right after Selkirk's disgrace, became fascinated by the implication of Sophie's battered eyes, and then he didn't fancy jumping a freight just when the weather was turning nasty. But their caginess made them bad bargainers on both sides. Neither man would risk an open declaration for fear of forcing the other's hand. They fenced at a great distance until December, and then settled the matter by dropping it. Chester was obviously remaining, and Alistair still wasn't paying him any wages.

But I was going to say that other than these business discussions, Chester still found himself alone from dusk to sunup as the weeks passed. And except for Sundays at church, his only society during the daytime was Alistair or one of the other brothers, who might drop around in the line of work. Mulling things over, Chester realized that if Sophie's face and her hobbling gait hadn't been such an embarrassment, the family might have let him sit in a corner of the kitchen every evening, just as they hadn't run him off their lawn during the summer. He could see how Sophie's vanity might be involved, and he was confident that Alistair must feel his wife's condition as a reproach against himself. Chester also imagined that husband and wife probably quarreled now, and didn't want an outsider to overhear. But if he understood all this, down in his forlorn cabin he still cursed them as inhuman, and cursed himself for caring. If you weren't a Wilson on our road, the isolation could sometimes feel crueler than anybody's tongue.

Besides, Chester had another private reason for wanting to get into the kitchen, the sort of reason which makes him such a powerful force in the family history. The whole Wilson phantasmagoria began to absorb him more deeply after Alistair had chased the preacher off and beaten up Sophie, and he would have liked as many more hours as possible each day to observe them all, but especially Alistair, eating or bouncing his little ones on his knee or unlacing his boots and spitting in the eye of destiny.

The kind of interest Chester now took in Alistair's family is indicated by some funny experiments he began to carry out. You might say that like any farmer, he was roused to new activity by the sounds and smells of autumn, for his little jobs were a twisted parody of the farmer's usual improvements. His projects weren't conceived in the ordinary spirit of vandalism, however; Chester got no pleasure from seeing a piece of lumber smashed for its own sake, nor was he trying to destroy Alistair's whole farming operation out of stupid spite. Rather, he arranged small challenges in order to see how Alistair would react. When would he show temper, when might he cry out in frustration, when could he smell a rat gnawing at his tranquility? Chester scattered his misdeeds about the barn and fields, taking care to divert from himself the blame for a hammer missing, a pig lost along the creek, a forkful of hay strangely spilled in the mud and trodden underfoot.

Chester wasn't sorry, either, to see Alistair spanking a child now and then as misdirected punishment for his sabotage. The injustice struck him as negligible considering all he had at stake, and it gave him a further chance to study how a Wilson wounds and how a Wilson suffers. Father and children, they were all Wilsons to him, and the name began to sound in his ears as if it denoted a species of laboratory animal.

Chester's curiosity does him credit, I think. Pondering the preacher's and Sophie's fates, picking up a rumor now and then about Claude's unyielding displeasure with Kate, Chester became convinced that the brothers' treatment of himself wasn't random, meaningless cruelty, like the cruelty he'd seen wherever men ran in packs in the freight yards and struck out at any interloper, defending their turf and spreading their chests like beasts to be admired. Granted, the Wilsons' violence, like their sense of humor, carried many of the same effects as an ordinary man's; but it was rooted,

Chester thought, in a fabulous desire. The brothers were cultivating a Wilsonian profile, which they intended to build up deed by deed and tale by tale until they achieved four heads as huge and solid as Mount Rushmore. And for the sake of that monument to their own glory, they appeared willing to risk any extreme—maybe even to the point of human life itself.

Their ruthlessness struck Chester like a fist in the gut when he caught his first glimpse of Sophie just after Alistair had walloped her. She pulled her lumpy, spoiled face back from the kitchen window as soon as she realized he was staring, as if she'd been a secret devil or a curse that a family hides to protect itself from being understood. But those few seconds were enough to start the ferment inside his head that led him to a kind of cankered moral certainty, and provoked him to those small experimental acts of destruction.

"Can they get away with anything at all, then?" he asked himself. "Doesn't it make any difference what other folks want, or who else comes to live among them? Are they dad-blasted gods of the earth?"

It was a reasonable question to ask, because affairs around the farm had now reached the point where only a supernatural immunity to normal causes and effects might be able to save Alistair from being humiliated in his turn. From the injured face glimpsed in the kitchen window, from the hired man's enforced exile at mealtimes, from the way Alistair eagerly sought his brothers' society for comfort every evening down the road, from the sudden sharpness with which he punished his little boys for crimes they hadn't committed, Chester gathered proofs that Alistair's fate must be rushing toward some stunning reversal.

Nevertheless, for a while the results of Chester's experiments around the barnyard were uncertain. Sure, Alistair lost his patience twice a week, bawled out the nearest person, slapped the haunches of any cow that got in his way, but when the episode was finished, the glass slivers swept up or the lost hammer found, he was still prince over his own dominion. In the evenings he returned to the circle of his brothers and reaffirmed his majesty. Chester began to suspect that he needed some handle to use against his boss that he still hadn't found yet, and only fate could put it in his grasp.

His thoughts hovered about Sophie. He wondered if the wife of a Wilson would tolerate her captivity forever, or was she wild to break out? Sometimes he could picture her creeping down the road alone clutching a carpetbag, and Alistair coming back at dinnertime to find her flown. Once as Chester replayed this scene in imagination, he saw Alistair even more furious than usual: an old Model A waited for Sophie by the bridge, to carry her off where the Wilsons didn't own the land and lay down the law. That would be a wonderful, a decisive test, maybe the best a fellow could hope to devise, but it was hard to see how Chester could ever bring it about. He hadn't exchanged a word with Sophie in five weeks, and he had no means of coming near enough to test the waters and do the persuading. Nor was he able to speak privately with Selkirk, so how could he convey the message that Sophie might be eager to escape? As he lay in his cabin at night, waiting for fatigue to block out the chill and carry him off to discontented sleep, Chester's brain followed these roads, one after another, to their dead ends.

Then one evening his supper was late because Alistair's sons had bloodied one another's noses over who was going to carry slops to the hogs, and it took awhile to separate them and get the hogs fed. Then the little girls proved too excited over the ruckus to obey orders, but kept running about the lawn, twirling their skirts and yelling, "Get your dukes up!" like their brothers had showed them. Chester stood in his cabin doorway, thinking how all the Wilsons were brought up bloodthirsty from the earliest age, when he saw Lindy traipsing down from the kitchen with his plate and cup. It was a long time since he had been near her, and the sight of that swinging walk sent his blood surging. He had no time to plan, didn't even remember to slick down his cowlick, but retreated into the cabin and rolled a smoke to steady his hands.

When she got to his door, she didn't see him at once and stepped forward into the shadow, saying, "Mr. Chester?" in a soft, flat voice. He was seated at his table blowing smoke rings like a grampus, and when she caught sight of him in the dark she gasped, sloshing hot coffee on her thumb. That scalded her so that she cried "Oh!" and rushed to set the food down. She stood examining her hand while he rose nervously to help. They were facing one another at close range, therefore, when the last smoke ring, which had been jostled by the sudden motion, miraculously composed itself and settled gingerly upon her chest like a frothy halo. They both noticed at the same time and, equally a miracle, smiled into one another's eyes as Chester swept it away with his fist. He said "Howdy!" in a low tone like the voice movie cowboys always used to address the schoolmarm.

She put her burned thumb to her lips and said "Howdy!" back. He exaggerated her injury and general sacrifice in bringing down his dinner, to which she truthfully replied, "I can't seem to get the hang of frying chicken, and the vegetables were already cold when I left the house, but Cousin Sophie makes me so nervous, sitting at the kitchen table all day giving orders faster than a body can jump and finding fault with every move I make, so it's no wonder the meals I turn out!"

Heaven knows what prodigious lies Chester might have uttered about those miserable half-cooked dishes if Alistair hadn't shouted down from the kitchen door, "We're waiting for supper now! Where'd you run off to?"

"Ow! I forgot!" she breathed, hurrying away. "They never let you rest for a second."

"Good evening, thanks again, good night!" Chester called

like any boy. She had spoken no more than fifty words, but he repeated every one of them to himself ten times as he devotedly gnawed the bloody meat from his chicken bones.

As the days passed Chester concluded that not all the interest lay on his side, because Lindy began to find excuses to run errands to his cabin. If none of the older children had washed hands yet, she brought the food down and lingered half a minute as he cut into whatever crusty half-raw mess she had concocted. Where whistling had failed during the summer, smoke rings succeeded marvelously that fall. Whenever Chester spied her approaching, he would quickly fill his room with them before she got to the door. His discontented thoughts about the Wilsons were absorbed and transformed by his new dreams of her, and those little seeming accidents he'd been planting around the farm ceased. Now he passed his evenings remembering her face, her mouth, her breathy soft words strung out in a country drawl that any man would have found sweeter than cherry pie.

As for the cause of Lindy's interest in Chester after months of ignoring him, I can only guess. He hadn't gotten any handsomer, though maybe steady eating had filled in his cheeks a bit. Probably it was the attraction of one put-upon, half-imprisoned underling for another. They had grievances enough in common now, and maybe just standing in the presence of a fellow sufferer, sharing complaints against the Wilsons with him, was like a breath of air to her. On the other hand, she might have lingered simply because she enjoyed half a minute's rest, and she answered his questions because that was easier than putting him off with evasions. But her reasons were an enigma to Chester then, and still partly mysterious to him years later, when he told the story of those wondrous visits.

In the beginning he didn't direct their conversations according to any plan. He asked questions only as a way of keeping her near him. Still, a lot of information came out about Sophie's injuries and disposition toward her husband, what her sisters thought of the Selkirk affair (Liza and Vera had paid Sophie a formal visit and noisily expressed their shock—Lindy had heard it all through the closed parlor door), what Alistair had told his brothers about that hypocritical preacher, and the rest. What's more, the whole family was using Lindy like an animal, she told Chester. "I got to do it all now. Chase the kids across the yard, stoke up the stove and cook the meals, grind the clothes through that wringer till my arm's ready to drop off. I'm like a regular housewife without the husband that goes with it."

Lindy's indignation was directed more at Sophie than at Alistair—a fact which Chester duly noticed but never quite absorbed. He was vaguely willing to share in her resentment against her mistress-cousin's tyranny. Yet maybe he was agreeing more with Lindy's sky-blue eyes than with her depiction of Sophie as an overbearing shrew. For he had come to see Sophie as another of Alistair's victims, and in one corner of his brain the wife had every right to grieve over her lot at the kitchen table every day. In fact, Chester's sympathy for Lindy was all the stronger because he seconded it with a similar feeling for Sophie. They were both Wronged Women, and they prompted him to start thinking about his duty to wage some Holy War against Wilson the Turk in their behalf.

After days of such dreaming, Chester awoke suddenly to his chance. He made a point of asking Lindy that evening, "Did your old lady ever drop a hint she might leave him for the preacher?"

"Oh lordy, she's never said that!" the girl drew back. "She just knots up her hands till she makes me feel like I'm going to pop, because her folks make her feel so bad. But I don't know what she might do."

"You think you could tell her something for me? You think you could wait for the right minute, when the two of you are alone, then tell her you heard that Selkirk hasn't given up hope! Don't say where you heard it from, just see what she says."

Lindy's mouth dropped open and Chester could feel that something about the idea excited her. After a minute her smile came back, deeper, more contemplative, as though she had been kissed in a special place. He flushed to see that he had pleased her. As she left the cabin she said very low, "Well, I guess I'll ask her if I ever find a good time."

Sunday was two days off. Now that Chester saw things moving on one front, he thought that if he bore down he might get them going on the other side too. In church he sat on the aisle where he could stick out arms and legs and be clearly seen from the pulpit. During each of the prayers, when heads around him were bowed, he flung his limbs out and back, out and back until Selkirk turned directly toward him and glowered. Then Chester screwed his face into a tremendous wink and formed his fingers into a pointed rocking horse that gestured back and forth from his own chest to the preacher. During the sermon he leaned his head far into the aisle a couple of times and tugged mightily on his earlobe until it stretched so far a rubber band would have broken. These exercises visibly aroused Selkirk. Each time he saw Chester contort, he raised his voice and pounded his pulpit to spend the energy, whether his words justified the emphasis or not. At the end of the service, as Selkirk marched up the aisle toward the rear door, Chester fell into a wild fit of coughing, so that the simple hired hand beside him began pounding his back solicitously.

After all the respectable congregation had shaken hands and Selkirk was about to disappear through his secret opening, he looked quickly toward Chester, who had been lingering apart from the rest of the farm help, and mouthed the word "Bridge!"

Chester stared back intently and repeated, "Bilge?"

Selkirk spelled the word out with his stubby finger upon

the black leather cover of his Bible, then quickly flung the door closed. Chester nodded and smiled.

But that night when he wrapped himself up and walked the back way by the creek down to the little stone bridge, no Model A was waiting. Nor on Monday, nor on Tuesday. Moreover, Lindy had not found an opportunity to bring any of his meals so far that week, so his mood had declined greatly from the euphoria of Sunday by the time, on Wednesday evening, he finally caught sight of the old car parked among the weeds. Selkirk was standing on the far side, relieving himself against the rear tire, dog-like, when Chester came upon him.

"Where you been all week? You'll get frostbite if you leave that out on a night like this."

"A devil's lot you care what I get! You turned them loose on me with pitchforks, after you'd told me I could take the Lord's own sweet time!"

"Darned if I could help it! I nearly knocked him down to keep him from walking back to the house, I wanted you to have it so bad."

"Here, look here," the preacher said, dropping his pants in back. "You see those welts?"

"Can't see a doggone thing in the dark."

"Give me your hand then. I want you to feel them. That's where they pronged me, there and there and there. Couldn't sit down for three weeks to save my blessed soul. Get your finger out of there!"

"I'm mighty sorry, I sure am."

"Sorry isn't healing my wounds any faster. One of them got infected and the doc had to clean it out. You know what that feels like on your bum?" Selkirk grunted, fastening his pants.

"But this time I got a foolproof idea! I can get you another chance with her!"

"Another chance to get my ass whipped."

"This'll be different. Now that she's been beat up herself, she'll run off with you for good."

"Run off! What'd that get me, you crazy loon? Where'm I going to take her? How'm I going to preach on Sunday if half the county knows I got a gal stashed in a barn somewhere?"

"But she's been smacked around real bad. I saw her face. She's crazy to get away. She'd die for you now."

"Well, I wouldn't die for her, so that's the end of that. You're God's own fool if you think . . ." Selkirk opened the car door and prepared to step inside. "Besides, I'll tell you something else. You know that little bird-beaked gal that plays the piano for the hymns?"

Chester nodded.

"She's a darned sight easier to get at than these Wilson women. Has time to cook, too. Lives right in town over a store. Simplest thing in the world, compared to driving out this road all the time." He climbed in and shut the door. Then he rolled down the window. "And another thing: my congregation's drying up because of these Wilsons. The collection plate should be fuller than King Solomon's mine this fall, the harvest these farmers had. But what do you think they're dropping in? Pennies, nickels, a couple of quarters. The Wilsons don't even reach in their pockets when the plate passes down their row, and everybody else takes their cue from that. They're trying to starve me out! Families that signed up to bring me a ham or a jar of preserves, now they don't show, the next Sunday they tell me they forgot. Weren't for that piano lady, I'd be skin and bones. All because of your hare-brained idea that you couldn't pull off!"

Chester grabbed the preacher's shoulder through the open window. "You hate those Wilsons just as much as I do then! We're brothers in this. We've got to make them bend. Now are you with me or aren't you?"

Selkirk looked at him hard and got down off his high horse. "Well, sure, heaven knows! Vengeance is mine, says the Lord, yours and mine. But I'm not going to slit my throat just so I can prick them a little. You want to pay the Wilsons back, you've got to figure out a better plan than running off with the wife."

"Oh, don't worry, I got lots of ideas. You can go after them a hundred different ways."

"Like how?" Selkirk asked squinty-eyed. "They never looked so easy to pick off to me."

Now Chester rolled his head about on his sinewy neck and the stars swept by and he gripped the preacher's shoulder tighter as the inspiration seized him. Maybe there *were* other ways to get at them. "Now, you take their land, for one thing. How do you think they got ahold of so much? You think they bought it? You think boys like that played fair and square?"

"Let me loose," said Selkirk. "How did they get ahold of it then?"

"Why, you can hear them bragging about it any day in the week. About how their pappy swindled it off a government land agent. Their pappy was an old snake in the grass, could talk you out of your last breath on earth. He rigged up some scheme, got somebody drunk, got six parcels of homesteading land instead of the one everybody was entitled to."

"That so, is that so?" asked Selkirk thoughtfully. "You know I wouldn't be surprised if that was a fact, or something like it."

"You bet your sweet Bible it is. Everything they've got's been built on a swindle, more or less. Some con game. You take that extra property old man Alistair farmed this year, his back eighty. Where you think that came from?"

"Where?" asked Selkirk, and from his tone Chester saw he had him good now.

"From his wife's cousins, the ones that lit out for California and left Miss Lindy behind. But I ask you, what could he have paid them for it—what kind of money's a farmer got in ready cash these days? And why's Miss Lindy staying here like some kind of slave, instead of going off with her family like any normal girl'd do, to help her ma with the young ones?"

"So how'd Brother Alistair get that land, then?"

"That's what you got to find out for us." Selkirk looked surprised, so Chester went on. "I can tell you what I saw and heard, what stands to reason if you think about it a minute. But the proof's in the courthouse. You know a lawyer you can trust?"

"What if I did?"

"He could look up the land titles for us. Then we'd know where things stood. We could make our plans from there."

"Suppose we find out everything isn't on the up and up, what good does that do us?"

"We can sic the sheriff on them! Doesn't the law apply out here just the same as in town? Don't Wilsons have to respect other folks' rights? Maybe they got to pay an extra fee if they're squatting on land that doesn't rightly belong to them. Maybe a smart lawyer could even take it away from them. Maybe they swindled those cousins out of the back eighty, and somebody'll have to go to jail. Or maybe"—the thought crossed Chester's mind for the first time, and he laughed high up in his throat for the love of it—"they'll have to bargain with us to keep it quiet. We'll let them have half, and turn over half to us. We'll maybe bring them to their knees, by God!"

Suddenly Selkirk twitched away and turned the ignition key. "I got to go. Somebody's fixing me a little supper right now in town. You tell me more about this tomorrow night. I want to hear every detail before I make a fool out of myself in front of a lawyer."

"What if you aren't here when I come?" Chester whined, anxious at the preacher's quick departure.

"Then you be here the next night. I'll come as soon as I can get away."

The car rolled off and the lights switched on. The fields were muddy, there had been showers on and off for a week, and when Chester got back to his cabin he had to clean his boots with a stick. It took him half an hour because he had the shakes, wondering if the preacher thought it was all a cock-and-bull story, or if he'd be back like he said.

The next night the Model A was parked a little farther up the hill on drier ground, and Selkirk was sitting inside it underneath a lap robe. He made Chester stand beside the car and opened the window only a crack to listen through. This didn't bother Chester. He needed the outdoors to move around in, to raise his arms and shake his fist and step forward and back, to spend his indignation and nod his head, grinning sometimes at the pleasure it gave him to nail down a point. At last he had a willing audience that might actually be influenced to some purpose, and he rose fully to the occasion that night, and the next and the next. Once he started recounting all the Wilson stories about how my great-grandpa had snatched an entire road's worth of land away from a homesteading agent, he took an almost Wilsonian delight in making the narrative flow. When he detailed his suspicions about Sophie's cousins and the back eighty, it sounded as though he had become a Wilson himself, thinking like one in order to unfold the sort of plot a Wilson might devise to chase his poor neighbors off and leave behind a girl to drudge for him.

Especially Chester was drawn to the image of my great-grandfather, that old trickster who, in Chester's imagination, began to seem more and more like himself. Both had come to Missouri landless and friendless, both determined to outwit and outwait the opposition and finagle a means of coming into possession. Both knew how to tell a story, and how to dream. It was the old man's sons who violated this pattern, for they had merely inherited what their pappy had won by hard-breathing treachery and guile. That's why it hurt so much when they lorded it over a fellow—they were swollen with brazen ego, yet they'd never needed to prove that they deserved what they possessed. After a while Chester began to regard the brothers as no better than squatters on their own land, while Chester himself was the old man's true heir. In the same way he somehow slipped into thinking of Selkirk and himself as kin, and a match for any other brotherhood on the road.

Now that he and Selkirk had become thick as thieves, Chester's only grief was that Lindy, once encouraged to sound out Sophie about an elopement, couldn't be stopped. The girl had evidently begun her own dreaming—either in sport or out of an interest in affairs of the heart, which were still new to her. Possibly she was also clever enough to realize that by helping her cousin run off, she would achieve the most perfect revenge for all that housework: Sophie would spend the rest of her life on the lam, accompanied by a pompous hypocrite. And if Sophie disappeared, Lindy would come into her own as the only grown female left on Alistair's place—though I can't say for certain she ever looked that far ahead. Anyway, on the evening before Chester's second conflab with the preacher, she managed to bring supper down to his cabin in order to announce, "Well, I asked her."

There was no putting the girl off. If she usually acted diffident and slow, on the subject of Sophie's interest in Selkirk she was bright-eyed and determined. Though she reported, for the record, "Cousin Sophie doesn't see how she could run off with a man she barely knows and leave her babes crying for their mother!" the real message was clearly the opposite. Sophie wanted the particulars and Lindy had been dispatched to collect them.

Chester managed to stall her for a day, protesting nervously that he'd have to ask for specifics himself, though in truth Selkirk had been so definite about refusing to consider the idea that he didn't see how he could bring up the subject with the preacher again. But the next evening Lindy returned to say that the delay had done the trick, Sophie's mind had turned, she would listen to a concrete offer. Chester was driven nearly frantic by the women's mounting pressure. But when he tried to weasel out from under, Lindy made clear how much he could lose.

"That's what I figured—you get us going, then you can't deliver."

"Sure I can deliver. I talk to him practically every day."

"That's good, because you know what'll happen if you can't? She'll tell her old man, is what. She'll say you were trying to steal her away, and then the whole family'll be down on you like a ton of bricks."

"I thought I told you not to say it was me that was asking."

"I don't have to tell her. Who else could it be, if it's not the preacher himself? Isn't exactly a crowd of folks passing through here every day."

"All right then," he flung out, racking his brains. "Tell her we're making plans right now. Tell her to start packing. Ask her how she means to get out of the house when the time comes."

"Aren't you supposed to get her out?"

"Hell no. Our side provides the car, your side's got to get her to it. The preacher's been stung once, he won't come up close anymore."

"I'll tell her," Lindy half-smiled. "Give her something to think about for a change. But I don't know how long she'll wait. She doesn't trust you much, anyhow."

In a way this threat didn't matter, because Chester was already committed to pitying Womankind under Alistair's domination. Although he had become interested enough in the shadiness of those Wilson land acquisitions as a consequence of talking with the preacher, he was still attracted by the greater intimacy of stealing his enemy's wife. Of course Lindy's threat *should* have mattered quite a bit; it should have taught him something about the women he pictured himself fighting for. But any threat coming from the female side of the household only aroused a greater compassion in him, and it was that motive, more than fear, that prompted him the same night to risk mentioning an elopement to Selkirk for the second time.

"By gad bejesus hosophat!" cried the preacher. "If you want to steal that woman so bad, take her for yourself! I told you I'm not interested!" He started up his engine. "If I find out there's anything in these land deals, I'll maybe help you. But that's all." The car lurched away.

"When'll you be back?" Chester called in alarm.

"Give me two, three days to talk to the lawyer. He might want to drive down to P'burg and check those courthouse records. When I know something, I'll meet you here." The headlamps switched on and the window rolled up. A drizzle had been turning Chester's clothes soggy for several minutes, but he stood still in the road, watching the little red lights on the back of the car disappear over the hill.

It may seem surprising that he was not more discouraged at Selkirk's rebuff of the proposition about Sophie; but Chester only lasted among the Wilsons at all because of his grit. On his way back to the cabin, he concentrated on rejoicing to think that Selkirk still believed in the land deals, anyway. It must have been all those Wilson stories Chester'd been telling, and the way he'd begun to imagine himself like my great-grandpa, for it seemed to him that at last he'd proven himself to possess the gift of gab. One of the plots he'd devised was already going forward. After that, it was surely reasonable to hope that luck or the sweep of events, which generally accompany the gab, would be with him. Maybe the preacher's lack of interest in Sophie didn't matter; maybe he could hurl himself into the storm and carry his second plot along too.

Next morning as he crossed the barnyard he saw Lindy on

the back step of the house beating a rug at a time when he knew Alistair was on the far side of a distant shed. Chester took off his hat and tossed it high in the air as a signal of success. It landed amid some pig droppings, but he didn't mind, since she saw and nodded, laughing possibly at his exuberance. She made certain to bring down his dinner. He told her, "In two or three nights, so be ready!"

She appeared surprised, and her half-smile modulated into a look of admiration. "She'll be there," Lindy said and walked off slowly, swaying at her hips like a little girl does when she lets her body loose, thinking deeply or daydreaming.

But how was Sophie planning to slip out of the house past Alistair? It would have been impossible except that most evenings her husband was still driving down to Tony's or Jethro's, where the brothers were congregating all that fall. Claude left Kate alone and came too, not so much daring her to further sin as to suggest estrangement. Only Liza and Vera, the faithful ones, were blessed with the men's company. Underneath their joking and storytelling, the brothers came together out of a profound worry. A doubt gnawed at their manhood, a fear that if they were four brothers, their wives were also four sisters, who might plot and scheme just as the men did. The brothers could not understand why any of their women would look at Selkirk, why they were not satisfied with their role in building up the Wilson dynasty. So the men gathered out of the need to fill a room with comforting presences, to listen to voices they knew they could trust. Even Tony and Jethro must have wondered if they'd been spared their brothers' sorrow only by accident, or if their wives were faithful by conviction and would cling forever.

Now when Alistair traveled to meet his brothers, he never ran into Chester and Selkirk down at the bridge, because Chester knew Alistair always left about half an hour after supper, so he didn't start out until later. And Selkirk never stayed long—the nights were brisk, and despite his growing interest in Chester's tales, he was anxious for the comforts of town. While Alistair, finding more reassurance in the company of the other Wilson boys than he could draw from the sight of his huddled, silent wife, always stayed out past nine. So that if Sophie planned ahead, she could be well gone some night before her husband discovered her missing.

She tried to escape three times in the following week, clutching her luggage and limping alongside Chester in the mud to the place appointed. But Selkirk was never there when they arrived, and after they had waited until the last possible moment before Alistair would be returning, Sophie, who had stood silent for over an hour, would sigh or sob or laugh or whatever that clutching sound meant, before she turned and picked her way back to the house.

Chester became more solicitous as his embarrassment grew. He urged her to sit on the bridge rather than standing between the tracks in the center of the road, looking into the blackness as though she could see all the way to town. He tried to persuade her to let go of her suitcase and purse a minute, but she hugged them the tighter when he spoke. Occasionally he offered an observation on the damp of the evening or the far-off animal sounds, but she never acted like she heard him. As they neared the house after the third night of waiting, however, she broke silence.

"I'll do this one more time and then I'm blowing you and him to smithereens."

She had already caught a bad cold, so her words came out muffled and choked. To Chester they didn't sound so much like a Wilsonian threat as the pathetic flailing of a woman he wanted badly to help, a woman whom others had mistreated and who might naturally lash out at him, as a representative of his sex, without really meaning it. He never feared her then.

The next night Alistair didn't go out. You can imagine Chester sitting down in his cabin waiting for his master's departure, as Sophie sat in her kitchen waiting for it, as Lindy poised herself for the sound of it. But Alistair, dumbly sprawled at the center of the house, felt too tired from his day's labor and fell to snoring soon after supper. Finally, just to make sure he didn't miss Selkirk and lose contact altogether, Chester slipped down to the bridge alone, but no one was there. What a relief, therefore, that Alistair hadn't left after all!

But the night after that, when Sophie did make it down to the bridge again, the Model A could be seen parked a few paces beyond. The moment Chester caught sight of its dark bulk he left Sophie and ran up, shouting, "Ho, Preacher, hey there, ho!"

As soon as Chester got close, Selkirk rolled down his window a crack and hissed back, "Keep your voice down, fool! What's that coming along behind you?"

"What's been holding you up? Did you see the lawyer?"

"I saw him. Who's that coming there? Who've you brought out to jinx me?"

"Hold on, hold on! I got wonderful news for you!"

"That looks like a skirt! You dad-blasted fool—" Selkirk turned the key and the car groaned into life. "I told you I wouldn't have any part of that. Now how're you going to get yourself out of this?"

The car pulled onto the road past Chester and began gathering speed just as Sophie came up, panting at the sound of the preacher's voice.

Chester called, "Wait! She's got something to tell you! Just talk to her!"

"Where's he going? I'm here, I'm here, Alonzo! Don't listen to that fool, I'm ready to go!"

The car was a good hundred feet beyond the bridge now and its little red lights soon disappeared like bloody stars over the top of the hill. Chester stood in the road looking after it with an indescribable feeling of pity and maybe fear knotting his innards. Sophie, still calling after the preacher, ran in pursuit as best she could, her bag thumping against her leg and finally tripping her onto her side halfway up the hill. At which point Chester bestirred himself and came to lift her out of the filth.

"Old Mister Hot-to-Trot!" Lindy called to him from the back step. "Mister No-Deliver!"

She never brought his meals down anymore, and he noticed funny things about the food the children were dispatched to his cabin with. Beans and beets might be stirred together and drowned in pepper. He would cut into a square hunk of meatloaf and discover it had been hollowed out and filled with a ball of catsup. The women seemed to save leftover coffee for his exclusive use and sent it out cold in the chilly weather. Desserts, which had been served up generously over the weeks before Selkirk had failed them, now disappeared altogether. Once in his potatoes he found a dagger-shaped glass sliver; it looked like part of a lantern he'd purposely broken at the barn six weeks before. The piece was too big for him to bite into by mistake, but it was clearly meant as a warning of what else they could do when they were ready. A couple of times, when the children apparently forgot to carry his meal, neither of the women reminded them, and after waiting an hour past his accustomed eating time, Chester had to go up to the kitchen door and inquire. When Alistair saw this, he raised his eyebrows but said nothing.

He was thinking, Lovers' Quarrel.

From the look of things, a person who didn't know about those nights waiting for Selkirk might easily have drawn such a conclusion. Alistair had already told the other brothers how Lindy had started spending a few minutes down at the cabin lots of days, and once when he noticed a bough of crimson leaves in the kitchen, he immediately assumed that Chester had brought it as a love token.

Now, if the pair had fallen to quarreling, Alistair figured that his big chance had come at last. It might finally be possible to stir up some fracas that would produce the great Chester-story the brothers had been waiting for. They were doubly eager at this point, because they longed for a distraction to take their minds off their wayward wives and the preacher.

At Alistair's prompting, Claude asked Donny why he'd stopped walking down to visit Lindy every night. None of the brothers had noticed precisely when Donny had paid his last call; they supposed it had been at the beginning of the new school year, when the youth didn't get back from Hickman until 4:30, then had chores before supper and homework afterward if he wasn't too tired. He still smiled at Lindy in church and might hope to bring her a chicken wing when the families ate Sunday dinner together, but she would take the wing gingerly, her eyes not quite focusing on his face, and she'd never say more than "Thanks!" It was not even clear that she knew his name, for she never spoke it. Donny must have told himself lots of things, just as Chester had done in the summer—that she was still virgin-green, that she was embarrassed to be seen spooning in front of the Wilsons. But whatever excuses the boy invented, the fact remained that she never showed pleasure at the sight of him. Consequently, though he didn't forget her, didn't find another girl at school to spark with, still it seemed he'd given up hope of winning her interest and waited in a kind of mooncalf's limbo.

So when his father inquired why he'd given up courting, Donny had no answer ready and could only blush, though his younger brother Horace piped up quickly, "Because she won't have him!" Donny threw a spoon at the boy, Claude laughed himself red in the face, and Kate rapped her knuckles on the kitchen table for order. Kate was having terrible headaches all that season anyway.

When Claude could talk again he said mildly, "I know somebody who's making time, if you aren't."

Donny was aghast at his father's information about Chester, and when Horace chuckled over his brother being outdone by such a rival, the youth determined to slip down to Alistair's and confirm this humiliating development.

When Donny knocked at the kitchen door, Alistair was just on his way out, but he decided a story might be about to unfold itself, so he took off his coat, pretending to be too tired to drive down to Jethro's that night, and settled in by the stove to observe the swain. Donny struggled to speak casually, including his aunt and uncle in his remarks about the wet autumn and the news of his high school class, but his torment quickly showed when he asked, in an unintentionally loud, squeaky voice, "What's old Chester the funny duck up to these days?"

Lindy, who was washing the supper dishes, gave a loud laugh, and even Sophie couldn't keep back a strange sound of scorn. Both Donny and Alistair were surprised at such strong expressions. As no words followed these outbursts, Donny drummed his fingers on the counter top and then, wilder than Alistair had dared to hope, he shouted at Lindy, "If you think he's better looking than me just because he's an old man, then welcome to him! Sure he's been around, he can teach you all kinds of dirty things I can't. Go ahead, live in a cabin and wash your betters' dishes all your life. Nobody else wants you anyhow!"

This was such rough language that Alistair felt he had to reprimand the boy for appearance' sake. But Donny didn't stay around to hear much, because suddenly Lindy broke out in hysterics and couldn't stop until she'd run into the bathroom under the stairs to wash her face. By the time she'd returned, her giggles under control but her complexion still slightly purple, Donny had left Alistair in mid-sentence, storming out the door for home.

After that the youth acted quickly. He was observed the next evening walking past Tony's and Jethro's on his way to Alistair's, though Alistair reported that Donny hadn't knocked at the big house. Did he hide in some brush, staking out Chester's cabin? Was he watching for Lindy to come outdoors so he could confront her privately? Or might he have lost his nerve at the last minute and retreated in shame?

Before the brothers could resolve these questions, Chester appeared at Alistair's back door the next morning with a wrinkled scrap of paper in his hand and asked, "This your idea of a practical joke?"

The note read, "Come out and meet me like a man."

"Must be Donny," Alistair told him soberly. When Chester looked confused, he added, "He must have found out about you spooning with Lindy. That young pup wants your hide." From inside the kitchen Chester heard a wild screech and then a crash, as though someone was shaking so badly she had dropped a cup.

"What you mean spooning? We haven't been spooning!"

"Doesn't matter to me, that's your own business," Alistair said. "But I warn you, Donny's whipped a lot bigger kids than himself at school, so he's in training. Best be on the lookout he doesn't jump you from behind."

Chester's eyes bulged and he turned back to his cabin without another word. His mind brimmed with new suspicions. Alistair might be egging him on over nothing. But more likely the women (burying their differences to become allies against him) had manipulated Donny into the role of their champion. Of course the youth was just beginning to fill out his frame like a man and didn't come anywhere near Chester's height, but heaven only knows what his father might have taught him about fighting dirty, if Donny actually did want to fight. The most aggravating thing was, the women had evidently tricked Donny into feeling jealous over an attachment between Chester and Lindy that had never existed. Chester found it maddening to think that he might have to pay for pleasures untasted—though wasn't that just the Wilson way of treating a fellow?

All day Chester stayed away from the shadows in the clear open air where he could see every movement around him, and when he got back to the cabin he opened the door warily, as though some beast might be hiding inside. But that was Friday, so Donny was at school and nothing happened. In the evening, though, Tony's whole family saw the youth striding toward Alistair's into a cold west wind. Again, nobody at Alistair's house saw him arrive, and Claude, who'd driven down to Jethro's to play canasta, didn't know what time his boy got home.

Next morning Chester found his door rigged so he couldn't get out of the cabin, a rope knotted around the handle and looped over a couple of boards in the eave directly above it so that only Alistair could free him. On impulse Alistair pretended not to understand the message brought by his little boy, who'd taken Chester's breakfast down but was unable to deliver it. So Chester had to stew inside until nine o'clock; before he got out he nearly wet his pants, since the cabin had no plumbing and he didn't keep a chamber pot or other crockery.

By the time he was freed, therefore, he was fighting mad. He lit out for the house, intent on confronting Lindy and discovering what she'd put Donny up to. He'd decided that if the women were hoping to settle his hash, he could play at treachery too—he could threaten to tell Alistair that Sophie'd kept a suitcase packed under her bed for a week, planning to run off the first chance she got.

But Alistair, seeing where Chester was headed, assumed

simply that he was planning to chew Lindy out for turning Donny on him, and he didn't want any of Chester's anger wasted in a shouting match with a girl. He hoped to direct Chester where the best show could be had. So he called out, "Whoa up!"

Chester turned, glaring, and Alistair came on fast. "She didn't have anything to do with it. I saw what happened. The boy came down here one night and asked her if she'd been waltzing with you. She just laughed at him. It's all in his head. He's the one you got to go after!"

Even though Chester was steaming, Alistair's words caught him up short. If a Wilson was encouraging him to do something, it must be in his interest to do the opposite. Yet even if Lindy had encourged Donny to hate him, still the youth *was* the one who must have tied the cabin door closed, and who knows what other hurtful plans his Wilsonian brain might hatch, now that Lindy'd made him mad? So Alistair might be offering good advice at that. Maybe Chester's wisest course actually lay in confronting the boy. He stopped in the middle of the path, trying to make up his mind.

"What'd Mr. Claude say if I beat up his son, though?" he asked after a minute.

"Who feeds you, my brother or me? I can't have you tied in your cabin half the morning and expect to get any work out of you. You better settle this or we're going to have no end of disruption. My wife's having trouble with the girl too. She keeps staring out the window half the day, wondering what Donny'll do next. Can't run a house *or* a farm while that kid's laying for you."

The mention of Lindy reminded Chester what a satisfaction it would be to show the girl how he could beat her pipsqueak boy-champion to a pulp. Suddenly he snarled at Alistair, "I'll be gone for a spell! Back at dinner!"

He started running toward the front gate, but Alistair called after him, "Wait up! If you're going to Claude's, get in and we'll drive together."

If Chester had been allowed to walk up the road to Claude's, the ending of this story might have been different. Striding along at a fast clip, that's enough distance in the brisk late autumn air to get a man's blood up, to make him ready. Chester could have charged into Claude's barnyard and found Donny sweeping out the feed shed and faced him down in five seconds, warned him against any more tricks, and the whole affair might have passed into silence, the brothers forced to admit that for once Chester had acted like a man. But sitting silent beside Alistair in the wagon seat all the way, Chester's energy didn't pulse into his legs; it settled in his stomach instead, where it churned uselessly while he fixed his attention on distracting little things that under-mined his courage. He noticed, as the wagon jostled past Tony's and Jethro's houses, that people looked up at him and grinned. No one saluted, but everyone dropped their chores and fell in behind as if they knew exactly what he was up to and were planning to watch.

When the wagon at last reached the top of Claude's hill, Chester had time to observe that Horace was on the look-out up a tree. As Chester watched, he shinnied down the trunk and ran to fetch Donny and his dad. By the time the wagon stopped before the barn, Donny was already there, his sleeves rolled up, his fists clenched, his jaw jutting. Claude stood behind, his hand over his lower face, but the marks of a broad grin pushing up the flesh just beneath his eyes.

Chester sat still a minute, though Alistair jumped down immediately, acting eager to lead the horses to one side so the story of Chester's battle with Donny could begin. Then Tony's and Jethro's kids began to pour into the barnyard. One boy shouted out, "Who brought a rope to make a fight ring?"

They seemed far more certain about what he'd come for than Chester himself. As he glanced about the barnyard, panic rising in his chest, he saw that he was being railroaded, that all his calculations had gone wrong. He felt fear like a shaft of steel in his innards over the way they might be planning to help Donny win, or how they might pummel him if he laid a finger on the youth. He had been a fool to lose his temper even for a second around these Wilsons. They could always turn your passion against you.

Donny, seeing that Chester didn't look very awesome as he clutched the wagon seat with both hands and stared crazily at the gathering family circle, called out, "I hear you're doing some courting these days! Come on down and tell us about it!"

The children mobbing the wagon picked up the taunt. "Who you courting, Chester? Who you courting? Is it Lindy?"

Claude dropped his hand from his face now and fixed Chester with a devilish smile. Tony and Jethro, who had come walking instead of running, arrived through the front gate and nudged one another when they saw the figure hunched on the wagon in the middle of the boisterous crowd. Tony cried, "You're bigger than him, Chester! Get on down and show him what for!"

Since Chester still sat frozen, Donny stepped forward and shouted again, "I say I hear you've been courting! That true?"

The children were screaming at his ankles and the brothers formed a line behind Donny. The horses showed their nervousness by lifting their legs and snorting. Horace, who'd climbed into the second floor of the barn, made a demon's face through the big middle window and called down, "Hayooo, Chester!"

"No!" all at once he screamed. "They told you wrong! I haven't been courting anybody! Nor there isn't anybody around here I want to court!" He jumped down from the wagon. "Nobody on this road's good-looking enough for me," he tried to josh them, heading toward the road.

Puzzled, the children stepped aside for him to pass, their smiles frozen but not fading yet, for they didn't understand at once that he was letting them down.

"I just tend to my work. I don't want any of your women-folks." He reached the gate. "Just my job, that's all I want. I love my job."

Donny looked after him, clenching and unclenching his fists and torturing his jaw. You could see that he was more nervous about Chester's departure than he'd looked before, when he'd been expecting to fight. Now there was nothing standing between him and Lindy; he had no excuse for not succeeding.

"Damn!" muttered Claude at last, his eyes following Chester's back. "Slipped through our fingers. What kind of story's that going to make?"

A very young Wilson, Stanley, looked up at Jethro and asked, "Not going to be a fight, pa?"

"Doesn't look like it, son. Not today, anyhow."

Stanley glanced around excitedly and ran over to his twin, named Marshall, who stood near the horse. "Put up your dukes!" he cried.

Next morning Alistair was surprised to see Chester appear scrubbed and dressed for church when he drove the wagon around to pick up Lindy and the kids. (Sophie still didn't go, pleading her health.) Chester had disappeared all Saturday afternoon, hadn't been in his cabin that evening when supper was brought down, had growled nastily at the kid who'd fetched his Sunday breakfast. Alistair wondered if he'd gone off to Hickman in search of booze, or if he'd started to run away for good and then changed his mind. In any case, there he stood, saying nothing but ready to hoist himself into the wagon as always. Alistair watched him from the corner of his eye and then, as they were turning into the road, said, "Morning!" as if the observation had just occurred to him.

Chester spat into the mud and grunted, "Morning!" barely loud enough to be heard over the horses' hooves.

But during the church service he became animated, swaying about in his pew like a restless sea. He wheezed and coughed and threw his limbs violently into the aisle; he stared at the preacher during the prayers and shouted out the hymns—which was all the more attention-grabbing because the row of hired hands never sang as a rule. Even the Wilson brothers noticed. "Looks like old Chester got religion yesterday," muttered Tony to his wife.

Everybody noticed, that is, except Selkirk, who kept his eyes lowered during the prayers and stared up at the ceiling throughout his sermon, as though not wanting to meet Chester's gaze any more than he wished to look into the faces of the congregation that was trying to starve him out. Nor did he pause when Chester tried to intercept him at the end of the service by stepping on his shoe. Chester sat stonily at the back of the wagon all the way home and refused to join the families at their weekly communal dinner.

Three more Sundays went by like that, Selkirk holding himself aloof. During the weekdays, the hired man brooded constantly over the humiliation of being forced to apologize to a fifteen-year-old boy. Nor was he cheered by the constant mockery that met him everywhere he looked. If Lindy crossed the yard with a bucket of water and Chester was in sight, she'd wave her slender arm as though welcoming a lover and call out, "Hello there, my beau, that fought to the death for me!"

The little Wilson girls, overhearing, would cry after her, "Hello my beau!" "Fight to the death!" "Chester's my dear dear beau!"

"She's just as much a Wilson as any of them," he began to tell himself. "If I fix the brothers, I'll fix her just as good."

One of his greatest fears now was that, if Selkirk's lawyer friend had figured out some way to settle the Wilsons' hash, it might involve restoring the back eighty to Lindy at Alistair's expense. Chester didn't want anything restored to anybody— he wanted it snatched away so punishingly quick they'd all think a tornado'd hit, and there he'd be, laughing at their incomprehension, their common misery, most of all at the justice of their comeuppance.

But why did Selkirk ignore him, when he hungered so desperately for revenge? During the long weeks between Sundays Chester pondered this question too, and crept out to the bridge more than one night to see if maybe the preacher had returned to deliver a message or even to bawl him out for having once brought Sophie along. Chester would gladly have submitted to any tongue-lashing, just so Selkirk appeared. But there was never a parked car, and though Chester lifted every rock in the nearby ditches, he found no note, no sign. It occurred to him once, walking back from that lonely spot, that if the lawyer had discovered some really promising case against the brothers, in which the accuser could be rewarded for bringing them to justice, that lawyer and the preacher might have decided to dispense with Chester in order to split the profit fifty-fifty. For Chester never questioned that a slick lawyer could uncover something on a bunch like the Wilson boys and their pappy. They'd rolled over too many folks to have left no legal trace.

The suspicion grew that he was being cut out. But how to make certain? Then a morning came when Alistair was driving into Hickman for supplies and suggested that Chester ride along to help him load the wagon. Maybe Alistair planned to bait him in front of the store clerks, or maybe he just wanted to observe him, for Chester had been pretty quiet the last few weeks, at first out of anger, then because his turbulent calculations about the preacher were distracting him.

Now, in the late autumn, Alistair always made the most of a trip to Hickman, stopping at the bank, sometimes at the agricultural extension office, and standing around the feed and grain to see if anyone might come by who'd offer a good tale to recount the next time he met his brothers. So it wasn't difficult for Chester to slip away while Alistair was jawing.

As soon as he could, he ran straight for the parsonage, but when he knocked, there was no answer. He might have looked next at the piano player's apartment, but he didn't know where she lived. He could risk maybe fifteen minutes more. He glanced up and down the street, not knowing what to do with his limbs. He started off toward the church one minute, turned downtown the next, then stopped again in the middle of the sidewalk. "Well tarnation, why not?" he asked, when he told this part of the story in later years. "I had to find out, didn't I? What had I got to lose?" So he steeled himself and strode off toward the little brick house where Bill Beagle kept his law office in those days.

I suppose old Beagle never had another such client as Chester marching into his inner sanctum past the typist in the outer room, leaving her speechless over the idea that such a wild and woolly fellow might have business with a respectable lawyer, let alone that he'd act so peremptory about it. Chester twisted the doorknob behind the secretary's back, and there sat Beagle himself, round and pop-eyed as always, cigar ashes scattered down the front of his blue vest, spluttering against the intrusion even before he'd gotten a good look at Chester's face. But Chester stood leaning over the desk until Beagle finally saw that he was immune to splutter. Then he asked, in that tone public men used to employ toward their inferiors, "Well, what is it, and don't be all day."

"Preacher been to see you yet?" Chester inquired tersely.

Now Beagle understood everything at once. This was Selkirk's source. He slowed down and acknowledged, "Yeah, we had a couple of words a few weeks ago. What of it?"

"Then you must've found out something about those Wilson land deals."

"Those Wilson land deals, as you call them, cost me the waste of half a day down at the county seat, my friend. If you're the crack-brained fellow that sent Reverend Selkirk in here, I ought to tan your hide. There isn't anything wrong down in the records office with any of those Wilson properties, unless you got evidence you haven't come forward with yet."

"Why, hell yes, I got evidence. There's nothing they talk about more than the way their pappy swiped all that land they're farming from a government agent, oh, sixty, eighty years ago. He was only entitled to one section, and he took six. Doesn't it say that in the deeds?"

"I'll tell you a little something about all those homesteading claims, friend. There aren't more than two or three of them between Ohio and Colorado that'd bear looking into real close, if you could actually get all the deeds and birth certificates and other documents together and compare them. But the courts aren't interested. The government wanted all this land settled, and as long as it's been legitimately occupied and no other claimant comes forward, there's no case against anybody. Possession's nine-tenths of the law; didn't you ever hear that down in the cave you crawled out of?"

Chester couldn't believe what he heard, so he asked again. "You mean the law stands on the same side as swindling?"

Bill Beagle formed his big round patronizing smile. "Not generally, but if the swindling went on long enough ago, the law takes a wink when it sees it coming."

I can imagine Chester gasping and flinging his arms up to clutch at his head over this news, but pretty soon he quieted down, remembering his other point. "Well, did you look up about those eighty acres Alistair Wilson stole off of his wife's cousins that lit out for California last year?"

"I took a glance at the title, sure."

"Well, what's it say?"

"Says it belongs to Alistair and Sophie Wilson since last October. Doesn't say why the former owners ran off to California, doesn't say why they sold to the Wilsons, doesn't say why they left behind Miss Lindy, that I see sitting with the Wilsons every Sunday in church. Deeds don't say much at all, in fact. It's mighty hard to use them as evidence against somebody unless you got lots of other evidence already."

"Like what else would I need?"

"I'm just speculating now, I don't know what the facts are, any more than you do, I imagine. But suppose pretty Miss Lindy was willing to claim in court that Mr. Alistair chased her dad off his eighty acres with a rifle. Or bamboozled him out of his property with some phony security. And then somebody else, like, oh, some hired hand around the place, had actually witnessed Mr. Alistair doing it and could back up her story. You got any evidence like that, or any chance of getting it?"

"I'm not sure. Maybe I saw something like that and maybe I didn't."

"Did you tell me you got to Hickman before or after the Douglases left for California?"

"I didn't say. I came here afterward."

"Well, then, that's swell evidence you got so far. When you find some better than that, come back. Don't come back before."

Chester didn't speak another word in the office. He stalked out past the typist, who followed him with her wide-open eyes. When he reached the sidewalk, though, he stopped dead in his tracks and looked directly up into the heavens, where thick gray clouds were racing along, bringing an early winter in with them. But Chester didn't see the clouds; he was looking through them to whatever lay on the far side. Finally he shouted aloud, "Isn't there any way they can be touched?"

Chapter Five

Winter hardened, and Chester declined from the full flush of energy and passion that regular feeding and intimate struggles with the Wilsons had aroused in him earlier that year. He withdrew into himself, and my grandfather, living down at the far end of the road, didn't see him again for maybe three months. After his interview with Bill Beagle, Chester made no further attempts to contact Selkirk; he stopped going to church altogether. Since Sophie didn't attend either, Alistair let the matter slide. Sometimes when the road thawed into a sea of mud, he stayed home himself and read a few Bible verses to the children instead. But no one ever thought to invite Chester into the parlor for those brief ceremonies. The fact was that he now appeared disreputable to a new degree, far worse than on that spring day when he'd arrived, bone-weary and stinking, to inquire after Claude's goat. As the year drew to its close, the hired man began to look as though he'd given up on himself—as if he was expecting to die.

The Wilsons attributed his decline to the combination of too few winter farm chores and his discovery of Harrison Grimshaw, the local bootlegger—for he was often trekking to the distant stand of timber beyond Alistair's back eighty, where the old still lay hidden. Alistair's boys usually found him swigging from a stone bottle when they brought his meals down to the cabin, and on weekends he generally refused all food, locking his cabin door with a stick on Saturday afternoon and not reopening it until Monday at breakfast time. Two nights and a day spent in that narrow room, the air putrid, his excrement and maybe vomit wrapped in a burlap sack, and two or three quarts of raw liquor consumed. Everyone said it looked like the beginnings of a suicide.

The family wondered where he got the money to buy the bootleg. Had he come to Hickman with silver sewn in his clothing, booty from some faraway crime? Or did he steal from my uncles to support his habit? But Alistair never discovered valuables missing, nor did he receive complaints from neighbors, so he was forced to assume the hired man's honesty.

More likely, the Wilsons decided, Chester performed some service in exchange for the drink, like scrounging firewood for Grimshaw's still, though you might prefer to think of him as paying with the actual results of the liquor—the fumes of wayward thought he conceived under its inspiration. Maybe, half-drunk already, he entertained old Grimshaw by telling him some whimsical plan for revenging all the Wilson atrocities by setting fire to their barns, or driving their cattle into the road some night and leaving the herds to wander away. He could have reminisced about women too, telling how they may smile and eat your heart in tiny bites.

Grimshaw himself was a tired remnant of Prohibition, taciturn, unaccustomed to such a fancy tongue as Chester's, and maybe susceptible to a strange excitement over the sheer fact that any fellow could talk so, not about weather and crops, or even in the usual manner of stories, but rather by pouring out grotesque impossibilities not meant to be believed, uttered to relieve a fierce pressure.

But whatever talking Chester did while he was under the influence, the words must have sounded crazed and disjointed, because everyone noticed that his mind was deteriorating rapidly. Children sometimes crouched beneath the cabin window and listened to him deliver rambling orations or lapse into curses. After a while he didn't bother to keep the words to himself as he walked outdoors either, so any-body might encounter him raging violently with some imag-ined adversary. He was often found disputing with the very person who discovered him. He told off Alistair and Claude pretty regularly this way, though once he was found address-ing Lindy in a slobbering lyrical voice, and he sometimes lec-tured the absent Selkirk on principles of religion. Naturally he was still making plans too, tossing his arms into the air as he dreamed of snagging his enemies in some fatal trap, while those enemies, as they watched him slowly limp across the yard and disappear, shook their heads with a dismay that was only partly feigned.

Once his drinking started, the brothers began remember-ing tales about alkies frozen to death on the steps of the Hickman hotel, and farmers bankrupted by the same vice. They hoped Chester would overhear and become enraged, of course, but their motive wasn't wholly malicious this time, for they were trying, in their perverse fashion, to rescue him through these warnings. Chester paid no heed to their stories, however, and for once his indifference wasn't pretended. He was caught up in a fantastic mixture of his own speeches and the fuddle of Grimshaw's poisonous brew, which left him powerless to concentrate on other people's voices. While the Wilson brothers remained important to his imagination, they had ceased to interest him in the flesh. If Alistair stood di-rectly before him, he might walk around the obstacle without focusing on its identity, unless his boss laid a hand roughly on his shoulder.

Meanwhile, the Wilsons were genuinely disturbed by Chester's ruin, though less over the waste of a life than out of regret for the loss of their climactic Chester-story. They could not regard his miserable disintegration as the great tale they had hoped for; their sense of proper narration involved winners as well as a loser, and if he drank himself into the grave, they could scarcely count themselves victorious.

But why didn't they intervene more directly, when by the end of January it seemed clear he wouldn't last till spring? The answer to that one is simple. Because Chester wasn't family, and their policy was never to stick their noses out too far.

Consequently the only Wilson who tried hard to touch Chester that winter was Donny. But this isn't a pretty story either, since after their aborted boxing match in the fall, Donny declined too. His parents noticed a new sullenness and the breaking of long-established habits. Claude refused, however, to admit that his son could be disheartened by a comical nonevent involving someone as low as Chester, while Kate still felt poorly, nervous as a cat and no longer respected by either of her sons after she lost her husband's confidence. So there was no one to prevent Donny from hanging around the Hickman school grounds till twilight, or drifting down to the pool hall where beer was sometimes served to minors. If he got home from town so late that he missed milking, Claude punched at his ears, but he wouldn't unbend enough to ask where his boy had been. Such a question would have implied the unthinkable—that a Wilson's son preferred some anonymous crew of ruffians to his proper society on our road.

Donny's new behavior seems so sad, not because he began to desert the family, but because he was running away from his failure with Lindy. That dogged Wilson spirit in him tried to deny her importance by seeking out her opposite. If he believed her fragile, demure, virginal, he chose for his new companions those dirty-fingered, foul-mouthed louts who hung around the high school fringes and spent their nights chewing tobacco and arguing over small bets. To Donny their society must have seemed like a liberation from his futile love and his family's expectations. They taught him disrespect, which quickly turned into a world-view, and they gave him a chance for power too. He discovered that his new friends, Amos and Speedy and Trenchard and fat, fumbling Polly, would follow anybody who mastered a few rules about playing them against each other. This was a skill his Wilsonian upbringing had prepared him to exercise, and besides, he possessed more resources than any of the others for devising malicious entertainments. His pals were town boys whose fathers worked for the railroad; they didn't have as much experience with their hands, or understand as well how a farmer's machines and tools could be sabotaged. While the normal Wilson impulse was always to build up wealth, that winter Donny took a sour interest in showing his gang how to destroy it. He became our only pure anarchist, the necessary family invert.

Once he became the leader, Donny evidently planned to divert his followers chiefly by tormenting Chester. He brought them out in Trenchard's jalopy a couple of nights on trial forays. They surrounded the cabin once and beat on washtubs and hooted, and another time they pelted Chester with frozen cow chips. Donny was making plans to jack one end of the cabin off the ground, but before he could find the proper equipment, his gang rebelled. I think that tells a lot. Because they didn't complain that Alistair's place lay too far from town, or that the jalopy was cold on a winter night. They simply found Chester to be the wrong kind of victim. They weren't spoilers the same way Donny was; their reactions fell into a more normal range. They understood that it's funny to steal some scraps from a well-established farmer by the dark of the moon, but it's not so amusing to rob the destitute. The way Chester walked blindly among their hurled cow dung, muttering to himself about some unrelated subject, actually made them feel ashamed. Only Donny had been driven so mad by his disappointments that he couldn't understand a feeling like that.

And yet I suppose destroying Chester wasn't the only thing on Donny's mind. On the night he led his band out to

Chester's cabin to break the icy stillness with shrieks and thumpings like the banshees of a drunken slumber, he actually left the others to make the noise and take whatever pleasure they could when the hired man's bloodshot eyes and slobbering chin appeared in the cabin doorway. Left them in order to slip away to the big house and hide in the shadow of the elm trunk, watching an upstairs window to see if her magical face would appear, curious or alarmed by the din.

꩜ You wouldn't expect Selkirk to possess any healing properties, or to go out of his way performing deeds of Christian charity, but he is the resurrector of my story. He brought Chester back like Lazarus from the tomb into the mixed promise of another Missouri spring. New buds, new schemes, new agonies—as Chester proved when somebody approached him in the proper tone of voice.

Selkirk's act looks the more like grace because Chester didn't summon him. The preacher sneaked down to the cabin out of his own volition, even though common sense would have told him to lie low and keep his nose clean. He enjoyed his comforts in the piano player's neat rooms over the Wall Brothers' store, and evidently the Wilsons were going to allow his lechery to pass without official complaint, so that next May, when all the Methodist preachers changed assignments, he could move to yet another new beginning in some county where the rumors about him had not penetrated.

Selkirk's problem seems to have been that, despite his best efforts at keeping his angry heart under control, he was tortured by the longing to take one more good shot at the Wilsons before he left town, in payment for the way they'd undermined his ministry there, and he wanted Chester to tell him how the land lay. He could have had no idea how far his former ally had declined; when he knocked on the cabin door and a gray sagging face appeared, he must have been thoroughly shocked. Quite likely he took a step backward and fanned the air in protest against the stench of liquor and digestion, then looked Chester up and down disgustedly before he said, "Why, you've had a fall, haven't you?"

"Yeah, thanks to you," Chester muttered, staring back impudently.

This remark seems to have aroused the preacher's ire, because instead of tramping back to his hidden car in disgust, he felt drawn to direct the blame where it truly lay. "Why, majestic sweetness sits enthroned! What're you saying, brother? Have I caused you any harm? Did I leave you open to attack by pitchforks? Did I bring out a woman that you had no place to keep, and that would've been nothing but trouble, and that you'd warned me against doing? Or did I fill you full of lies about property that hasn't been stolen, and send you to a lawyer that laughed in your face? By great Jehovah, every time I listened to you I got creamed! I'm a fool for coming back now!"

"Then go on off," Chester said, reaching inside for his bottle. "Who needs you? This time I got me a foolproof plan, and I aim to carry it out alone."

He stumbled against a chair, which brought Selkirk inside to help him stand. Somehow the door closed, and the two men sat down by the lantern, exchanging countercharges and ill-tempered quips. The first time Selkirk took the bottle he looked distrustfully at the rim where Chester's mouth had sucked, and rubbed it with his sleeve before drinking. But he hadn't missed Chester's reference to a new plan, so he was apparently lingering until he saw what was up. Pretty soon Chester understood that the preacher would be leaving Hickman in a few months, which meant that an epoch was drawing to an end. On his side this naturally awakened a desire to exploit the present configuration while it remained in place. Although he had a drunkard's confidence in his own unaided powers, he also must have realized that along the Wilsons' road he would never find another conspirator, so he began weighing in his unsteady brain the improvements that might be made in his scheme if he took advantage of Selkirk's unexpected willingness to help.

Even though Chester never directly admitted it to me, the preacher must have been the decisive force that provoked him to act on his final grand design. He claimed he was just waiting for the nights to warm up so there wouldn't be as much hardship once he switched into high gear. But before Selkirk appeared, he was too dizzy-headed even to draw up the long list of supplies he'd need, and surely too weak to lift all the weight that would be involved. When the preacher first talked to him, the whole business was no more than a groggy half-baked idea, wouldn't it be wonderful if . . . ? Selkirk was surely the catalyst; he brought Chester a good ways back to reality just by sitting across from him and demanding that all his words be pronounced clearly enough to be understood. After the preacher did grasp what project Chester had formulated, he shook the hired man even more by crashing his fist down and declaring, "You're crazier than a coot, probably too drunk to be salvaged! I'll be back tomorrow night for one more try, and you'd better, good Lord in heaven! be sober or nobody'll ever bother to lift you out of the grave again!"

That tough talk made the difference, because the next evening when the preacher dodged from shadow to shadow down to the cabin and lightly tapped, Chester answered pale and sick from laying off the booze for the first day in two months. He bent over to hold his belly in both arms as though it was a bad wound; he couldn't speak more than a few grunts; in fact, he must have looked as though he wouldn't last through the night. He needed days to dry out completely, to hold his head straight without shaking and remember what somebody had said well enough to answer decently. But in spite of the pain, he stopped his boozing cold. You talk about grit, once he made up his mind!

This was probably the only week in Selkirk's ministry when he hung on a sick man's recovery with real concern. Indeed, if I was telling his story I might dwell on the sacrifices he must have made to drive that ten-mile round trip every night from Hickman, abandoning the piano player's cozy chair to sit in a bad stink and solace himself with nothing more than a few slugs from Chester's last bottle. And the chance he took in being caught by Alistair! Think what a roughing up would have occurred if he'd been seized on Wilson property a second time. How he must have stared at Chester's miserable sagging face, thinking his attentions were most likely wasted, his mercurial partner now irrecoverably useless. That impossibly grandiose plan of revenge Chester had spouted the first night was proof his brain had gone soggy. The more you think about Selkirk's side of it, the more uncharacteristic his persistence appears; except that he too was held by the dream of an eye for an eye. The Wilson boys didn't sit lightly on some people's souls, and in this Chester and he *were* kin, just as the hired man had said the previous autumn. If there was any chance of doing them dirt, Selkirk wanted in on it; if not, he was still attracted to the ceremony of indignation in which fellow believers confessed to one another that the Wilsons' arrogance affronted other folks' right to rise.

A further explanation for Selkirk's fascination with Chester is that he could not, apparently, come up with any plausible anti-Wilson scheme of his own. This sounds strange in a fellow gifted with such powers of verbal invention. But Selkirk's talent evidently did not extend to the realm of action. Confronted by a need to move in the physical world, he had so far been able to think of nothing more ingenious than cruising our road and knocking at the women's doors behind their husbands' backs. While Chester, as Selkirk must have realized, possessed a power of original creation—even the mad way he talked on those winter nights, still partly crazed by bootleg, showed that his brain continued to throw off conceptions far beyond Selkirk's ingenuity. The trick, Selkirk seems to have decided, was to get Chester sober enough that his imagination might be disciplined. Then the preacher could scrutinize his wild thoughts carefully and select from them some few usable scraps that might provide a really workable scheme.

This was a perfectly sensible way to proceed, except for one thing. It didn't take into account Chester's obsessiveness. The fellow was utterly incapable of tossing off plan after plan, waiting for someone to tell him which one sounded more workable than the rest. By the time Selkirk reached him, in fact, Chester's mind had been made up for several weeks. As he saw it, only one means could satisfy all his particular demands for vengeance against the Wilsons. So when the preacher attempted to establish a larger range in their discussions, Chester merely unfolded one arm from around his gut in order to point a bony finger and declared, "It came to me like a kind of a dream. I was looking up toward the big house from down at the pigpen, and the missus stuck her head out the back door to scream at the kids, and her whole body seemed to swim over the side of the house, like she was an apple bobbing in a river, or a cloud running across the sky. All of a sudden I saw the truth: nothing around here's nailed down. Everything's movable, if you just know which end to pick up first. Been thinking ever since about the best way to prove it. I decided what I got to do's snatch both them womenfolks. After that, it'll all come tumbling down. I've been figuring it out for days. Easy as pie. So if you want to throw in with me, fine. If not, good-bye."

Chester never quite claimed that he'd planned every step of his strategy in advance, or that he knew precisely why, against heavy odds, the kidnapping would have to work. I'm not even sure this was an important line of thought to him. He viewed the matter more fatalistically: not that success lay in the hands of the gods, but that holding Alistair's wife and servant-cousin for ransom had simply presented itself to his imagination as a single complete stroke, uniting his interest in the women, his hatred for Alistair, and his desire to win some important possession that would put him on equal footing with the Wilsons, so he was bound to make the attempt. The very chanciness of the undertaking conformed, after all, to his flattering image of himself as my great-grandfather's true heir. Part of his dream about the mighty heroes of the earth involved their ability to throw themselves upon an enticing wave and ride it in to shore. He knew the Wilson boys had done that sort of thing repeatedly, just as their pappy had before them. He still did not understand all the forces which could divert the wave, once underway, and break it to right or left, bringing you in gently or else cracking your skull, but he knew he would take the risk once more.

As the evenings passed and Selkirk noticed that Chester kept reverting, in his lucid instants, to the theme of snatching the wife and the maid, the preacher began to work up arguments against the craziness so they could get on to something more promising. "For one thing," he rejoined, "your stupid plan means carrying off two live-wire females. That means surprising them, overpowering them, transporting them, storing and feeding them for the duration! And Lord almighty! you never know how long it'll take to get the Wilsons to pay up! After a while you'll run out of canned pears for the gals to eat, and how could you slip down to check on them every few hours, to stop them from trying to escape or sending up smoke signals or screaming to folks passing by?"

Chester only replied, "Taking care of the gals'll be half the sport. I've thought about that part more than any other."

Chester was planning to wait until Alistair left to join his brothers down the road some night, and then grab both women as they were cleaning up the kitchen. He would tie them like two sacks of flour. "You can carry Sophie," he offered. "That way I won't have to make two trips. Doesn't matter how much they scream, since nobody within a mile will hear except the kids, and they'll be too scared to interfere. If you want, you can wear a handkerchief over your face," he added, though personally Chester wanted the women to recognize him at once. He wanted to see their expressions change when they realized he hadn't come this time to beg for anything, he'd come to sweep them up.

"Why, they'd battle us tooth and nail and hold us till Brother Alistair got back! Then I'd never preach again! Bishop'd throw me out on my ear the minute he heard about it. Plumb ridiculous. Even if the sheriff wasn't called."

But the stupidest aspect of all, Selkirk seems to have thought, was Chester's insisting on the deed to those eighty acres behind Alistair's farm as ransom. "You planning to scoop that dirt into your pockets and carry it somewhere else and spread it out again? Hell no! It'll sit for all eternity right behind the Wilsons. They're going to look at it every day. And if you're standing on it, they'll be looking at you. Of course most likely they'll just turn you over to the law for kidnapping, but suppose they treat you like they did me: string you along, watch you squirm while they wait for a chance to sock you back harder than you could ever hit them. Even if they give over that property and let you work it awhile, you could never rest. The night after you harvested your oats, they'd raid your barn."

"I'd raid theirs right back!"

"But that doesn't matter," Selkirk shook his head scornfully, "because you could never get possession in the first place. Why should they think a couple of womenfolks are worth the trade of eighty prime acres, when they love owning land more than they love their own souls?"

"They're men, aren't they? They know the value of a skirt just as well as you and me. They'll be glad to sign over that deed when the time comes. What I need you to do is tell that lawyer to get the papers ready for when I need them. Ever since I saw Beagle I've been thinking, he was just putting me off because he didn't take me serious. Those lawyers can always get what you want if they know you've got the dough to pay their fee. Al Capone never had trouble finding lawyers to jump through hoops for him."

"Al Capone, hell!" Selkirk spat. "What're you going to pay Beagle *with?*"

"Once the property's mine, I can take out a loan on it, can't I? A hundred bucks. Eighty for him, twenty for you. For being my messenger to him and for looking in on the ladies sometimes, when I can't get away."

Chester wasn't interested when Selkirk suggested a quick theft and then high-tailing it. Nor did he care to contemplate vandalism on some grander scale than he'd practiced before, because secrecy and speed were antithetical to the effect he craved. He planned to watch the gradual unfolding of his vengeance episode after episode. He wanted to be suspected and feared for a while. He anticipated gloating when the brothers finally discovered they couldn't touch him. And if things turned out right, he hoped to hang around for all eternity, just across the back fence, feet planted firmly on his own ground, waving cheerily to Alistair—his equal at last—while they harvested their matching fields.

"What if I won't help you? How'll you get Beagle to fix up the deed?"

"Let the Wilsons hire themselves a lawyer, and let them pay whatever it costs. Take awhile longer than if you get the papers for me in advance, that's all."

But something kept drawing the preacher back to hear more absurdities: the fascination of the Wilson outrage, no doubt, and the secret appeal of Chester's crazy, ambitious design. It couldn't possibly work—every one of Selkirk's arguments sounded ten times stronger than Chester's fuzzy reasons why he might pull it off—but there was something magnificent about the audacity. It was, after all, exactly what the Wilsons deserved. There's no question in my mind that these secret planning sessions marked the approach of Chester's finest hour, when he stood on the verge of seizing the initiative from his enemies and making them dance to his tune. I can well believe that Selkirk found his wild eyes and sweeping gestures irresistible.

Until the night the preacher noticed that Chester had stacked several cans of fruit and vegetables in a corner of the cabin. Next to them lay a pile of old burlap sacks scrounged from someplace and a five- or six-foot length of rope. Selkirk must have asked himself if he'd been dreaming the nights away, not noticing that while their arguments circled round and round, March had arrived and Chester was already gathering his supplies for the snatch.

His mind must have drifted off in a sort of terror until Chester asked him sharply, "You bring me that newspaper?"

Selkirk had stuffed the morning's Saint Joe *Gazette* into his overcoat pocket. He drew it out and handed it over. "What you want with this?" he asked suspiciously. "You planning to read it?"

Chester grinned. "I might. But afterward it's where I cut out the letters for my ransom notes. By the way, you got a pair of scissors?"

"One pair, at home. Can't spare them, though. Use them in my work all the time."

"Never mind, never mind, I'll get some my own way. You know, when the action starts up, you aren't all that much help."

Selkirk departed visibly panic-stricken. After that night he didn't return to the cabin for a long while. Now Chester was of two minds about the preacher: possibly he was devoting himself to the lawyer end of the plan and would show up again whenever the transfer-of-deed papers were ready. Or maybe he was as gutless as he seemed. In that case, Chester supposed, the initial stroke of his success in the abduction might draw Selkirk back into orbit. For when Chester was pursuing a goal, he was never prey to fundamental doubts. His only worry was that without the preacher, he might be able to haul off only one of the women. When the time came, he would have to decide whether to hit Alistair harder by choosing the wife or please himself more by snatching the girl.

My great-uncles put it another way. They said Grimshaw's whiskey contained some poisons that had killed part of Chester's brain and kept him loco for a while even after he sobered up. They claimed that if you met him down at the barn during that month when he was stealing supplies for his plan he'd always be packing some mysterious bundle under his arm and shuffling sideways to hide it, and he'd grin at you in a coy, flutter-eyed way and say ridiculous things like, "Morning, Mr. Alistair! Pleasure to see you down here!" As though he was fooling anybody about his pilfering. The Wilson boys knew many of the specific items that were missing and had discussed the matter together for several evenings running. But they didn't interfere, because they wanted to see what else would happen. Claude remembered a story about a couple of piglets that had drowned themselves in a creek once after licking up a pool of Grimshaw's corn liquor. So he wasn't surprised at Chester's carryings on. He just prayed the family wouldn't lose too many more goods before the drunkard finally strung himself up. By now the brothers had virtually abandoned hope that Chester could still deliver any notable story before he expired.

꩜ The first note was discovered thrust into the crack between Alistair's back door and the sill, just above the knob. Alistair opened the door into the frigid early morning blackness on his way to milk, and the folded envelope fluttered like a dead bird to his feet.

He was still puzzling over it when his wife came downstairs a quarter-hour later. "What's this mean?" he started to ask her, but she interrupted shrilly, "That girl's gone from her room, and it looks like the bed wasn't slept in!"

Alistair's head was swimming now, what with this peculiar message fashioned from cut-out newspaper letters and Sophie shouting at him about a bed not slept in, so he took several minutes to establish that the note might be connected to the girl's disappearance. The paper only said, "I got her. now ain't You in a perty kettel of fish. wait for next letter with ransum demand." At the bottom was a kind of three-pronged sooty splotch that might have been a bird's footprint.

Comprehension was followed by incredulity. Neither Alistair nor Sophie had heard any sounds during the night; they felt sure that when they'd gone to bed about 9:30, Lindy was in her room. Alistair was too agitated to remember his chores that morning. He drove down to see his brothers as soon as he could get the team hitched. Tony and Jethro met with him in Vera's kitchen, and a child ran off to summon Claude. The three puzzled over the note, taking their time to figure out where the letters had come from and debating what the phrase "ransum demand" might imply. Pouring them coffee, Vera muttered, "That girl always was a lazy slut anyway."

At last Claude blew in. The others looked to him for some wise pronouncement. But after he'd grasped the situation, he only said "Hmm" and sat down at the head of the table to think. Their inability to know which end of the business to pick up irritated them all. After a minute the elder three began to throw a lot of intemperate charges at Alistair, who found himself having to deny that he'd given Lindy cause to run off; and he was forced to swear he'd never discussed the back eighty in her hearing, so she couldn't be riled up about that. "We all agreed to keep the deal secret, didn't we? I haven't even told Sophie the exact terms!" He whispered this, because Vera was sitting in the next room.

Then Claude asked, "What about that drunken hired man of yours?"

"He's down at the barn feeding the cattle like always, I reckon."

"You got something missing and you haven't checked to see where the biggest thief this side of Saint Joe is?"

Alistair acted sheepish and backed out of the kitchen to go look. No one accompanied him, because Claude said it might arouse suspicion. Alistair returned in half an hour. Chester had been located in the barn, sweeping out the horse stalls. He'd already fed the livestock and brought the full milk pails up to the house. Sophie'd said he'd worn a funny grin and inquired if his breakfast was going to be late.

In the end they couldn't bring themselves to believe he was responsible. They had no reason to connect his recent petty thieving with a bold deed like this. He'd been so down at heel all winter that they'd stopped looking at him carefully, and it hadn't struck them that he'd begun washing himself again and shaving every Sunday, or that he didn't smell of liquor now when he spoke. But even in his better days last fall they wouldn't have wanted to imagine him capable of confounding them this way. That would have amounted to putting him on on equal footing with themselves. Preposterous!

Finally Claude announced, "I got work waiting for me up the road," and headed toward the door.

"But we haven't settled this thing yet!" called Alistair anxiously. "What if the gal's really been kidnapped?"

His expressing it that way allowed Claude to achieve a sudden perspective. "So what?" he grinned. "That's nothing to keep a man from his dinner." They all tasted the Wilsonian flavor of this joke and laughed harshly. They broke up their meeting with the satisfaction of having mastered the affair with their irony. But all through the rest of the day the puzzle nagged at them, and nobody could relax before the next note arrived.

That night by unspoken agreement the brothers were drawn by the mystery to meet at Alistair's house for the first time since Sophie had sinned. She didn't miss her opportunity. She served cobbler and coffee and she pressed seconds on them all. Alistair had forgotten what kind of hostess she could be; he looked toward her proudly and didn't order her upstairs when the men got down to business. So she had a further chance to capitalize on the affair by saying, "Lindy's the one to blame, whether she's run away or not. Even if it's kidnapping, isn't that proof what a wandering, aimless soul she's got, that just invites men to carry her off?" Sophie didn't fail to point out the contrast between her own steadfastness and such unreliability. She kept asking, "How could any girl desert a decent home like this to take up the life of the road?" Alistair, much comforted by his slices of cobbler, felt no disposition to remind his wife that she had recently shown a wayward streak herself.

On the strength of her virtuoso performance that night, Sophie began her rehabilitation as a family member—a process that was speeded up, in the following days, by her increased importance as the only woman left on Alistair's farm. Her husband couldn't shout in to Lindy, "Tell the missus I'm going up the road." He had to tell the missus himself, and that contact produced its sweet fruits. Moreover, Alistair could not spend all his day discussing Lindy's strange disappearance with his brothers, so he began to converse with his wife over meals in order to work out some new theory that had crossed his mind. Previously Sophie had not expected that her situation in Alistair's house would ever improve. I'm not even sure, before Lindy vanished, that she consciously desired any change. Sulking and resentment can be their own rewards, so she might have called herself satisfied with her discontent. Nevertheless, the kidnapping proved the finest opening she could have wished for. Within ten days Liza and Vera were acknowledging her reinstatement as an equal, sending her messages and jars of preserves as favors.

I might add that Kate also observed the way the brothers had begun hanging around Sophie's kitchen in the evenings and took her cue from her youngest sister. One day at dinner she asked Claude, "Just exactly what did that kidnap note say?" Before long husband and wife were drawn into a deep discussion. Claude felt himself strangely solaced by that meal and stopped brushing coldly past his wife whenever they passed in the house. The other Wilsons noticed that two weeks after Lindy's disappearance, Kate rode to church with Claude for the first time since the previous fall. By the third week the middle sisters were referring all their conjectures about Lindy to her superior judgment, as if Selkirk had never driven down the road to pray.

Now Sophie's recovery was furthered by the fact that for a while, no evidence arose challenging her contention that Lindy had caused her own disappearance. This was because Chester, as part of his cunning strategy, wrote no second note for four days. He noticed, of course, how the brothers were now meeting each night at Alistair's house. He grinned prodigiously over this, taking their eagerness to sit near the scene of the crime as a tribute to his powers. He luxuriated in their confusion, fancying that he could play them like a fisherman plays a trout, leaving them to dart off on a dozen wrong tacks before he jerked the hook in deep with a sudden cruel motion.

Meanwhile he attempted to overhear their evening deliberations by standing underneath Alistair and Sophie's kitchen window in the mud. He could make out the rise and fall of voices, could even distinguish different speakers, but he picked up nothing of substance. However, he was becoming cocky because Alistair as yet showed no sign of suspecting him. In fact, the boss had innocently asked him, on the first afternoon after the kidnapping, "You see anything funny around the place last night? Looks like your girlfriend's run off." Chester had ducked his face to hide a grin over that.

Still, his pleasure in trying to eavesdrop gradually fell off, so on the fifth morning another note appeared in the crack of the back door which cast much doubt on Sophie's theory. It said, "She is ok so far, wont hurt Her if You do as I say. if Your prepared to hear and meet My Ransum Demands, tie handkercheef on lightening rod and wait for next note." Again the three-pronged black splotch like a chicken track appeared at the bottom of the sheet, this time accompanied by a caption: "My mark, don't answer no letters without this."

That strange last line seemed to imply that Lindy's kidnapping was being covered by hundreds of newspapers across the country, and there was danger of crank letters turning up to be confused with the real ones. Chester appears to have read a lot of snatch accounts without comprehending the purpose of certain ritual details.

Tying the red cloth to the lightning rod atop the barn caused Alistair much trouble, because he had to borrow Jethro's extra-tall ladder to reach the roof, and that ladder was lying under several tons of hay in Jethro's loft. Ironically, Chester was sent over to help dig it out, but he didn't mind too much, since it gave him a chance to bait the two brothers by asking, "What you want a ladder for? You planning to paint a barn or a shed in this rough weather?" He was especially pleased to have thought up this trick that cost them a day's labor while further postponing their discovery of what ransom would be asked. "Playing them like a trout!" he muttered to himself.

As for the brothers consenting to be humiliated by tying up a bandana in Lindy's behalf, that's entirely out of their character if you suppose they acted merely to rescue the girl. I believe that when Claude scoffed at her, on that first morning, as utterly insignificant to the Wilson scheme of life, he was perfectly reflecting the family's attitude. What's more, Sophie's willingness to use Lindy's absence for self-advancement shows that even the girl's closest friend—the woman she had aided in the desperate Selkirk escape plan—saw no reason to stick up for her cousin once she disappeared. No, the only explanation for Alistair's climbing that ladder to reach the lightning rod involves the family's pride, and their love of climaxes. With the arrival of the second note they realized they were dealing with someone besides Lindy, who intended to challenge their manly wit, and in such a contest they regarded the girl as chattel. She was worth the effort of playing out a story, exactly as they would have played for a couple of hogs or a peck of peaches.

But when Chester demanded, in his third note, which appeared two days later, the eighty acres which Alistair had taken from Miss Lindy's family, he also put himself under suspicion for the first time. Because only somebody from the neighborhood would know enough about family affairs to connect Lindy with the eighty acres, and to remember that they made a separate parcel from the rest of Alistair's farm. That ransom demand certainly ruled out the wild theory that a stranger wandering through the county had decided to seduce or capture the first girl in the first likely farmhouse he passed, and hold her for a quick bundle of cash.

However, knowledge of the eighty acres only narrowed the suspects to folks living in the vicinity; Chester was the obvious candidate for several additional reasons which occurred to the brothers once they put their minds to it. Already as Alistair was climbing the barn roof with a red kerchief in his hand, he was thinking that, despite Sophie's assertions, nothing he'd seen of Lindy suggested she would go to such lengths to inconvenience the family. Of course she had her mysterious side, but her langorous, shiftless manner hinted that if she ever did run away, she'd never bother looking back. Whereas Chester, though decayed from his prime, had proven himself a restless schemer; moreover, of all the outsiders in the world, his familiarity with family routines made him the most capable of picking a suitable moment to carry off the girl in secret. And now that Alistair thought about it, Chester had a special motive for victimizing her. He remembered the conclusion he'd come to last fall: Lovers' Quarrel. He quickly saw that if you've got it in for somebody, one delicious revenge might be to subject her to all the frights and discomforts of being snatched.

So when the ransom note arrived at last, Alistair didn't take long to develop his new theory and he wanted to confront Chester immediately. But Claude said, "Wait awhile. He's playing with us, we'll play with him. Finally he'll give himself away—whereas who knows how much beating it'd take to get a confession out of him? And then if he didn't squeal for a long time, maybe the gal would starve before we got to her." They would consider it a defeat, technically, if they recovered her dead. "Or suppose Alistair's wrong?" Claude argued—though nobody regarded that as likely now. But just in case, they should give Chester no reason to complain to the law about rough handling. While a farmer wouldn't be arrested for disciplining his hired man within reason, any complaint would draw some deputy to snoop around the place for a morning, and that might lead him to uncover the fact that Lindy was missing. After that, the family might never regain control of the situation. When Claude finished laying out these arguments, Jethro and Tony nodded soberly, so Alistair bit his lip and agreed.

That night Chester was surprised to see Alistair appear at his cabin door with a letter. The boss said, "I'm supposed to play pinochle at my brother's, and this here's got to be delivered, so I thought you could take it."

Chester stared at the white envelope, which was addressed in large letters "To the Kidnaper." He gulped and said, "Sure, where's it go?"

"Can't rightly remember," said Alistair casually. "Probably doesn't matter anyway. Just stick it someplace obvious. You could put it under a rock by the road, I guess. Or in the mailbox, or work it through the barn door latch. I got to get going." He walked off to hitch up the team.

The letter burned in Chester's hand. "Wait!" he cried. "Doesn't it make any difference where I put it? Something as important as this must go in a particular place."

Alistair turned around slowly. "Why, how important do you reckon it is?" Then, since Chester did not reply, he added, "Doesn't seem so very important to me. Anywhere'll be fine."

As soon as Alistair disappeared, Chester tore open the envelope. Inside he found a ratty paper with some child's penciled scribblings of the multiplication table. On the other side a scrawl said, "We don't own those eighty acres. Also the girl isn't worth it. Like you say, we will only answer notes stamped with a chicken foot." Chester was already regretting the chicken foot business, because he had lost both feet and feared he would have to swipe another fowl before he could write the next note.

But that was only one of the worries piling up on his head. That cussed Selkirk had never showed up with the legal papers or to offer help in caring for the victim, a failure that was turning out to be more inconvenient than Chester had expected. The business of attending to Lindy was getting mighty onerous, because suddenly Alistair began keeping him unusually busy for the slack season. Where were all these chores coming from, that nearly prevented him from finding a single moment to slip off to the abandoned farmhouse on the back eighty and check on her, locked in a filthy bedroom?

Besides that, the girl had begun making difficult demands of her own. She wanted clean clothes from her closet in Alistair's house, and a wash basin, and some plum preserves from Sophie's basement shelf, and the new Monkey Ward catalog to read. And why couldn't somebody come out to visit her for a change, maybe Donny? Or else one of Sophie's children might be blindfolded and brought over secretly to play for an hour; that wouldn't hurt anything, would it?

Chester was driven almost mad by these proposals. The initiative seemed to be passing from his hands into hers. Finally he did manage to swipe a few jam jars from the basement, but none of them turned out to be plum, so he discovered their contents poured in Lindy's slop jar the next afternoon, after all his risk to secure them. He was so infuriated he nearly threw the whole putrifying mess in her face, but something restrained him. Something was going on between the two of them, which may have started on the night Chester carried her off. The fact that the preacher wasn't around to help with the abduction meant not only that Sophie was spared, but also that the relationship between snatcher and victim was bound to become an intimate—and not entirely hostile—struggle almost immediately. Chester found himself—against his will and better judgment—partly enthralled by the girl all over again, and in his confusion unable to resist her idlest request.

I cannot imagine that on Lindy's side the interest was equally romantic, and yet there were certain strange signs. After days when she carried her back up higher than a cat's, she could suddenly melt . . . For instance, what was Chester supposed to think of the fact that she succumbed to his entreaties—with a blushing giggle—and wrote for him, as a special favor, the next note to the Wilsons? The message was pure fiction; for she reported in her wandering little girl's hand, "I am ok but will be kilt if you dont turn over land like he say. Youre Cousin Lindy Sue Douglas."

I have been contemplating this brittle, yellowed piece of paper—a souvenir preserved by my Great-aunt Sophie—for some hint of what was really going on in the girl's mind as she formed the words. But all I can discover for certain are the faint food stains, the odd angular pattern of multiple folds, and the awkward three-pronged mark at the bottom which was Chester's attempt to draw the mark of a chicken foot, using his own finger dipped in some soot from a wick. The design is quite irregular, bursting into extraneous pools and shoots, and each prong terminates in a wide blotch. No wonder the Wilson brothers laughed so hard when they saw it, and at first voted unanimously not to answer the note at all. But then Claude got a better idea, so next morning Alistair handed Chester another letter, instructing him to deliver it anywhere he pleased, which said, "We have just rec'd a note with a forged stamp on it. Look out, you have got competition, and he may beat you up when your sneaking around at night."

That evening at supper Sophie informed Alistair that another of the hens was missing, and husband and wife exchanged a heartwarming smile of conspiratorial intimacy. Between them, it felt just like the old days again.

Chapter Six

🕸 Off in the peeling, unfurnished Douglas house that stood among five lonesome elms, the girl was free to see things her own way. It's not so hard to imagine some of the stories she might have told.

"Lordy, just listen to that wind howl. Comes in around both windows and through that crack in the pane. Sure sends those dust sluts across the floor in a hurry. They all keep company over there in the corner, like they were sisters. 'Howjado, Miss Dust Slut.' 'I'm fine, howeryou?' Like they were wearing big puffy cotton skirts and skittling around on tiny toes, each with a nasty bug after her to get tangled up in her parts.

"Could probably break out of here if I wanted. Nobody knows your own house like you, even if you haven't lived in it for months. Could pop that south window open in two shakes. He just drove a couple of nails in the sill kitty-cornered to hold it down. I've got out of worse. Pa used to lock me in the room across the hall sometimes for messing around with Lula instead of doing my chores. 'Now girl,' he'd say, 'you'll stay in here till tomorrow with no supper.' Fifteen minutes later I'd be whistling on the lawn. They couldn't ever hold me if I didn't want to be held.

"Jiminy, but that stove doesn't put out much heat, does it? He thinks he's so smart, got everything about this kidnapping figured. 'Here missy, I laid in tin cans for you to eat, and here's your stove wood, and here's a fine mirror to make yourself pretty in, and here's a pile of sacks to sleep on.'

'Well, so what?' I said. 'Where's the can opener? Where's the matches?' That first night was awful. Next day he ran clear back to his cabin and then no matches to be found, and he couldn't figure out any way to steal some from the big house till afternoon. And what was I doing all that time? Sitting here with a pile of burlap over my head and still not warm.

"This stove's not a heck of a lot better even when it's working. Would heat ok if he'd laid in some decent firewood instead of twigs. And this pile of grass, praise the Lord! Would you believe he thought a pile of grass would warm this room for a week? What he doesn't know about living you could write a book. Then every time somebody tells him he's been proved a fool, he turns red as a beet.

"At first you think that blushing looks real sweet, shows a man's sensitive, different from the way those Wilson men turn purple whenever they see a skirt flapping in the breeze. I swear, they walk by the laundry on wash day and kill themselves laughing over a couple of shifts. He doesn't laugh though, just ducks his head and his cheeks puff out, shy and tender like he was a little boy, brought a daisy to his teacher. That's how looks will lie. Nearly wrung my throat that first night when he grabbed me, till I told him to quit. Gentle my eye! I'd just as well have been a dust slut and twenty boots stepping on me, for all the gentleness he showed.

"I suppose it'll be in all the papers, like those snatches over by Jeff City the time Pa bought the paper when we were in town. 'Miss Lindy Sue Douglas taken from her bedroom. Present whereabouts unknown. Please inform police of any clue.' Just think about that. Rich folks you never heard of, reading your name at breakfast. Put your story down for the dog to eat his bone off of. Blowing in the wind, what's that to them? At least I never had my picture made, so no cat's going to pee on my nose. That's one blessing.

"Wonder how long till the cops start combing the fields to find me. If they call in the cops. But you got to call them, otherwise how do the newspapers find out? Bet those Wilsons'd like to handle this case themselves, though. Beat him up good, once they find out he did it. Probably kill him and throw him to the hogs. Wouldn't that be a loss! Sorry world, he's done for. Never gobble like a turkey again. Never snatch another girl, hold her in a stinking room, choke her and freeze her and starve her, like he did me. What a loss, world.

"Wish he'd come though. He stays away till I'm almost lonesome in spite of myself, just for anyone to ask me if I've eaten, or look me over to see I've combed my hair. You don't have somebody around for half a day, you start letting down. When that silly Donny was coming every night, him that I didn't care about, still I'd spend twenty minutes over the wash basin, scrub scrub scrub on my hair, turn myself out just like those pictures of the movie queen. Doesn't matter how hopeless or ugly he is, you got to have some man on the place, tell you what you're there for. Not this old Chester, though. He couldn't tell you because he isn't even sure himself. You say, 'Hello sir, I'm a woman.' He'll say, 'Well that beats me all to heck, which end's your front?'

"There, I hear him coming up the hall. Put this lock of hair behind my ear so my brow shows, even though I don't care if he notices."

She would have told herself stories day and night to fill up that empty room. It was the first time in over a year that she'd had so many hours to think about where things stood or to hear the sound of her own uninterrupted voice.

"I was standing in my little bedroom like always, drying my hair before the mirror. Cousin Sophie only gave me one candle to see myself by, but the light made me look sort of pretty, my hair glowing against my cheek if I stood just right. I was looking straight in my eyes, sort of dreaming. Then out of the blue I heard the door creak. Thought it was little Kermit again, wanting to sit in my lap till he fell asleep. Turned around, there was old Stringbean, his eyes big as saucers. Pounced on me before I could make a peep. Clamped a hand over my mouth, poked his other hand round my chest, so he could feel my nibs through my shift. We just stood there, him trembling against me, for three or four minutes, me wiggling to get comfortable and then trying to get my arm out so's I could pull back my wet hair.

"Feels sort of nice, a man's hands on you, after you get over the shock. He'd washed them, I could smell the soap all over him that night, first time he ever smelt of anything except tobacco and sweat. Only once he'd got ahold of me, he never moved, so I kind of snuggled against him with my behind, my crack parted over his leg back there. We both got to breathing pretty hard from the pressure, and he ran one thumb around my little nib just over my heart. One, two, three little circles he made. Could feel the roughness of his clothes on my shoulder too, but didn't mind that either.

"But his other hand was almost cutting into my jaw, where he was trying to gag me, so I shook my head loose and whispered to be a little gentle. 'How'd you get in?' I asked, and he said, 'Crept up the front stairs. The missus is in the bathroom scrubbing herself and couldn't hear me.' 'Then you haven't got much time,' I said. 'Let's get down to business. I'll be quiet.'

"Should've got my tipoff from the way he stared when I said that. How'd I know he hadn't come for kissing and cuddling, he just wanted to carry me off and lock me up in this cold house for days on end? A man pokes himself into your bedroom after he's looked you up and down for months out of the corner of his eye, how're you going to know he's got something else on his mind besides the normal thing? Sometimes you'd give anything to try it, and you wouldn't care even if they were old Stringbean's lips. When little Kermit puts his behind on my leg and starts jabbering away, his fingers stray over my tummy, I think, what a waste! Now you play all over me, when it doesn't matter, but ten years from now, when you'll have strong hands and whiskers sprouting on your chin, then you'll never look at the housemaid, won't even recollect who I am.

"So instead of cuddling, old Stringbean hoists me over his shoulder and carries me downstairs, past the bathroom where Cousin Sophie's splashing around, and before I know it we've reached the front porch, me still wearing nothing but my shift and my wet hair about to turn to icicles. 'Where we going?' I ask him, but he just shushes me and says, 'You promised not to talk. Do I have to gag you?' 'Well, at least give me some cover,' I says. 'It's freezing out here.' He says, 'I got a horse blanket down at the cabin you can throw over you.'

"Now I think we're going to his place so we won't have to be quiet about it and can take longer. Then I'll sneak back to my room after the family's gone to sleep. But when we get to the cabin, he just tosses a blanket at me and then it's up on his shoulder again, across the fields to this old place. Finally I see where we're headed, and I think, 'Well, he's going to a lot of trouble for me, but if it gives him a charge to carry me back to my own home and lift me across the threshold like a groom, I don't mind, even though it's awful cold. We'll warm each other up pretty quick once we get started.' But when we get inside here, he just throws me on the floor and says, 'There, missy, nobody'll find you now.' Then he backs into the hall and locks the door, panting heavy all the time from carrying me, and before I know it I can't hear him outside anymore.

"I cried out then, I was scared to stay alone here in the dark, not knowing what mysterious thing he had in mind. I sat down on the pile of sacks over there in the corner, half froze to death, and I couldn't think of anything except, 'Has he gone crazy? Will he come back to kill me in the morning?' I wanted out bad then, but I was so nervous I couldn't think to jimmy those windows and crawl back to Cousin Sophie's. Couldn't stop my teeth from chattering, till I pulled all those sacks over me. Finally about dawn the feeling went away so I could sleep.

"Next morning when he came back, I hid behind the door. He found me out, grinning like a rusty old hound dog. I said all trembly, 'What you going to do?' 'Do!' he says. 'I'm holding you for ransom, that's what! They're going to pay through the nose to get you back.'

"I busted out laughing, out of relief partly. He let go my wrist and I crimpled onto the floor, heaving around and couldn't stop, over him being so stupid. 'What's the matter?' he says. 'That's ridiculous,' I said when my voice came back. 'They wouldn't pay a plug nickel for me. They'd rather leave me out here to freeze than come looking for me.' But he was so ignorant he got all het up, saying, 'That isn't true, you're their relative, and you got the prettiest face around. Even if the womenfolks wouldn't ransom you, the men will.' 'Well, let him think so,' I said to myself. 'What difference does it make to me? It'll give me a few days' rest cure anyway, before the Wilsons beat him up and I have to go back to my chores.'

"But still, after I saw he wasn't going to touch me anymore I read him the riot act about the stove unlit and me not being able to open those tin cans. 'Look, my skin's blue,' I said. 'If you want to kill me there's faster ways than freezing.' After I saw how embarrassed he got, I figured we could mostly run things my way, so I set in handling him. One time he comes in here, I prance up and give him a surprise hug, then I dance away and laugh. That bowls him over, he doesn't know what to do with his arms, like if you give little Kermit a peppermint stick, he wants to say, 'Thank you ma'am,' but he can't get his mouth to make a word, he's so joyed. Then I step back and take a look at old Stringbean and I say, 'Sure would be nice if I could have some roast beef, I get awful tired of these canned vegetables.' That throws him in a worse tizzy than he was in before. 'Roast beef!' he says, scratching his big old elephant's ear. 'How'm I going to get you any roast beef?' I say, 'Should have thought of that before you brought me out here.' Off he goes, kicking the clods all the way out of sight over the hill, he's so discouraged to think he's let me down after I hugged him.

"Next time, to throw him off, I keep away in a corner and I really lambast him. 'You think they're going to let you get away with a stunt like this?' I tell him. 'They're going to tie you up by your Adam's apple and toss the body in a ditch for the birds and tell the sheriff you were thrown from a wagon. And nobody's going to care enough to look into it.' He tries to laugh that off, says, 'You claim they won't ransom you, but they'll kill me for you, is that it?' 'You know them as well as I do,' I answer right back. 'That's just what they'll do.'

"Last few days, he's been sneaking down here after dark just to talk about how it's going. He's afraid they've figured him out. Started wondering how he can ever escape from this business alive. Last night he asks me, would I tell on him if he just took me back to Alistair's on the sly like nothing ever happened? Honestly, he can be so simple. As though they wouldn't twist my arm out of its socket to get the answers, whether I wanted to tell on him or not. 'You could say you were blindfolded,' he tells me. I just busted out laughing at that, so he slunk away like a scolded dog.

"He hasn't laid a finger on me since that first night. So wrapped up in his stupid ransom notes, and what he over-heard one of those Wilsons say to another, and he's dreaming of how they might be getting ready to turn over some deed or other to him. Now I'm just an ear for him to talk into, or some prize for him to keep away from the other fellow, to make him pay up. If I'm so doggone pretty, like he says all the time, then why doesn't he take some interest in me for my own sake?

"That kid Donny knew what he wanted me for, at least, even if he didn't know how to get at me past Cousin Sophie. That's what I'll say tonight when old Stringbean comes. 'Why don't you bring Donny around, so I can have some fun for a change? Being held for ransom isn't the liveliest joke in the world, you know. I could use a pair of calf eyes to cheer me up.' That'll get his goat all right. 'Aren't I taking care of you good?' he'll say. I can see his mouth falling right now. His cheeks will just peel off onto his throat before I'm done. It's like having a doll face made out of mud: one minute you can draw the lips up, the next minute you can draw them down, happy, sad, happy, sad, like they were dancing legs and you called the tune."

ᑫ That spring Chester crept about the muddy fields at secret hours, tormented by his hopeless love and his dream of revenge. He was shielded by the unusually gloomy weather, which kept normal folks close to their houses or barns. The thick gray atmosphere and heavy shadows obscured vision so that on some days a man vanished within fifty steps. Scurrying and groping, he sought some avenue around the impasse that had grown up in his ransom negotiations and some way to descend from the maddening teeter-totter he rode with Lindy.

His excursions were complicated by Donny and his gang, who also made unannounced forays through the countryside that season in search of some mysterious end. Chester had observed that they no longer persecuted him at his cabin, so their immediate object in the fields must be something other than himself. The first time he stumbled upon them, they were holding a low-voiced conference behind a hedgerow, evidently arguing about directions or strategies. He retreated in fear before they noticed him. He supposed Donny had learned about Lindy's disappearance from his father and was beating the bushes for her, as any young swain might do, hoping for a reward from his scornful beloved. Clutched by his guilt, Chester naturally figured that if Donny ever observed him skulking about, the youth would see at once that he was Lindy's kidnapper, on his way to visit the victim, and lay into him mercilessly.

In fact, my Uncle Claude never mentioned to Donny that somebody had been kidnapped that spring. Now that the boy had become a truant and prodigal, his father did not trust him with such an important secret, and besides, Donny scarcely lingered at home long enough to overhear any news. He could only find distraction for his tortured imagination among his roughhousing friends. So it was more likely that Donny was poking about the fields because he was still enough of a lover, even so late in his decline, that he kept closer tabs on Lindy than anybody suspected, and had noticed for himself that she was missing. If so, he may have been conducting his own search independently of his father and uncles. But in light of the climax to Donny's story, it's also conceivable that the gang was merely scouring the countryside for old Harrison Grimshaw's still, hoping to steal it or else tip it over, since they thrived on that kind of pointless vandalism. Regrettably, my guesses about Donny can't be verified, since he disappeared from our road in the aftermath of the story I am telling, and I never met him.

Following that first disturbing near-encounter with the gang of ruffians, Chester learned to keep a sharp eye out through the mists and early twilights of the season. As he made his way over the obscure, soggy back fields, he was forced to creep as silently as an Indian, to watch for tracks in the mud like a scout, and to lift his head occasionally, listening for predators like any scared animal. He had reached a stage of continuous horror and near-despair about the kidnapping anyway, and the presence of these young destruction-prone demons made his pulse race all the more.

But a far greater worry arose from his stalemate in negotiations with the Wilsons. Once the note-trading started, both sides corresponded voluminously. Nearly every night through March and the first half of April, the brothers met to decide on the wording of their next reply, and to each of these notes Chester usually responded by the next morning. Perhaps not every document has been preserved, but the first summer when I came home from college I managed to collect, from Chester's grimy souvenirs and from the pasteboard box in my Aunt Sophie's attic, a total of twenty-four letters sent by the Wilsons and twenty-nine by Chester. The number of papers alone is sufficient to indicate the depth of the standoff, the gradual buildup of Chester's frantic wonder over the way he had been sucked in, as well as my uncles' fascination with the powers of note-writing to needle their enemy. I doubt they had ever before felt so convinced of the usefulness of literacy.

One other impressive statistic about all these notes is that five chickens eventually lost their lives to provide Chester with the feet he used to stamp his signature. Though the weather was cool enough to prevent them from turning rank for several days, they soon curled up so tightly that they became useless for making an intelligible imprint. One of Chester's periodic chores, therefore, was to slip down to the chickenhouse brandishing his pocketknife. With these wasteful deaths on his conscience, it's no wonder he seldom slept and his face grew more haggard as the kidnapping dragged on.

Of course, the most obvious difficulty involved in the note-trading was Chester's fear of being nabbed when he slipped up to the kitchen door at dawn with his answers. In fact, it would have been so simple for the Wilsons to wait inside that door until they heard a noise, then open up and seize him, that he could only have escaped because they decided they didn't want to take him this way. They were clearly in no hurry to end the episode, because they knew that Chester

was suffering more than they were from the delay, and besides, a rainy spring is a slow season on a farm. You have
only your livestock to occupy you until the fields dry out
enough so you can get your plow into them; consequently the
Wilsons had ample leisure to enjoy the diversion Chester
was providing. Their official story, however, was that they
were waiting for him to lead them to Lindy. They always said
they were afraid he'd clam up and allow her to rot in some
hole if he was captured apart from her. "Or if we'd grabbed
him," they used to say, "he might've shaken us off with some
excuse, like he'd found the note blowing about the yard and
he was just delivering it to its proper place. Then how could
we have proved he was lying?" they asked, winking.

But didn't their refusal to catch Chester at the kitchen
door compromise Lindy's safety? Weren't they worried that
she might already be hurt or starving or dead? Didn't they
wonder if Chester was capable of such violence, since he was
still little more than a disreputable-looking stranger to them,
after all? No; you see, for the Wilson boys there was no question worth considering, except whether or not they could
force Chester's story to the most spectacular climax imagin-
able. In other directions their brains just didn't function.

And what could the two sides have discussed in their many
notes? The more they wrote, the more topics of dispute they
uncovered. The brothers raised all sort of protests against
Chester's ransom demand—legal, social, even philosophical.
Their sophistical temperament was roused by the question of
whether or not Lindy was worth eighty acres; it was left to
the kidnapper himself to point out that "a life is a life and its
up to you folks to save her." They frankly wondered what
the kidnapper thought he could do with the deed, even if it
was somehow legally conveyed to him. Did he imagine he
might escape the law if he proposed to sell or—what a ridiculous idea!—farm the land himself? But on this point Chester's
confidence never wavered: "You won't call sheriff when you

see me standin in my corn field, cus itd gall you to much to admit you was took by somebody. Youd rather have me around to aim pot shots at." Over and over they protested that they didn't actually own the land Chester was after; Alistair was only holding it in trust for Lindy's parents, who might return from California at any time. Chester knew from Lawyer Beagle that this wasn't true, but he had no luck shaking them off their lie.

When all this wrangling bored them, the brothers reverted to their other favorite theme, their demand for elaborate proofs that Lindy still lived. In reply to this question, Chester at first offered anecdotes about her condition, which the brothers naturally refused to credit, since Chester might have been inventing them. The Wilsons expressed satisfaction only when Chester persuaded Lindy to write a note in her own hand, dated and describing the weather for that day, in which she affirmed her physical soundness through the laconic phrase, "Im OK but bein kidnaped is no piknik."

To bait him, the brothers occasionally invited the kidnapper to call at the farmhouse for face-to-face discussions. But this offer always sent Chester into a panic; invariably he responded that he was tired of waiting, that they could either turn over the deed tomorrow, or he would break Lindy into tiny pieces and scatter them over Alistair's lawn. Threats like that got him nowhere, of course. The Wilsons' next note read, "Go ahead."

One of the worst episodes arising out of the note-trading occurred because Alistair, who had been handing his envelopes over to Chester with instructions to post them anywhere he liked, got the idea one evening of asking his hired hand, "Just where've you been stashing those letters so the kidnapper always finds them?" Chester mumbled something about the elm stump in the pasture beyond the barn. Alistair said, "My brothers and I've decided to stake out the place and collar him next time he comes for a pickup."

The story which followed carries the inevitability of any good Wilson tale. The brothers solemnly handed Chester their next note. Under their eyes he conspicuously inserted it between folds in the stump's bark. Throughout the evening, one brother after another took his turn sitting under a nearby shrub with a rifle in his lap. Of course, the kidnapper never appeared; Chester was cowering inside his cabin, cursing because he was unable to pay Lindy a visit that night. About eleven o'clock, Alistair knocked on Chester's door. A drizzle had set in. Alistair ordered Chester to take his turn at watch under the dripping shrub. He was not given the rifle, but was told that if he saw anyone approach, he should hoot like an owl. Chester made a couple of practice hoots under Alistair's instruction, and then was shown where to sit. Alistair went up to bed. Chester crouched in the wet cold till dawn, his teeth chattering. He wished, during those hours, that he had never jumped off the freight at Hickman, that he had never walked down our road, or that he had possessed enough sense to turn back when my grandma had served him a plate with two measly biscuits on it his first morning. When Alistair finally came down to inquire what he'd seen during the night, Chester looked blue in the cheeks, though his ears were a stinging red. His bones ached so that he hadn't the strength to claim he'd caught sight of anyone snooping around for the note; the paper was so soggy anyway that it disintegrated in Alistair's hand when he tried to retrieve it from the stump— so what self-respecting kidnapper would have wanted it?

In short, the correspondence was getting Chester nowhere, but he didn't know how to break the deadlock and he had no one to advise him. Though he enjoyed talking at Lindy in a giddy adolescent way, the two never seriously exchanged opinions, but rather moods or vibrations. Their greatest intimacy occurred on the five nights when he brought over the chickens he had just killed for their feet. Lindy roasted the corpses on a spit suspended above her little stove and then the two fugitives shared a late feast. They established a sort of domestic routine built around the regular appearance of these birds every week or so—though their settled arrangement was often interrupted by stormy periods when Lindy claimed she hated him, and even once refused him entrance to her room for twenty-four hours, calling through the door that he was "stupider than any dead rooster!" But whenever she cooked the hens, the two almost-lovers squatted across from one another as though they were sharing a wilderness cookout, munching contentedly. Her nearest approach to a gesture of affection occurred on such a night, when she took a rag and wiped the chicken grease from Chester's chin without speaking a word. She settled back on her haunches while he stared at her then, smiling to herself.

Indeed, most of their happiest moments passed thus, silently. As for conversation, he told her how the ransom business was progressing (or failing to progress), and she followed his meaning more or less, depending on her level of interest at the moment, while she watched for a chance to demand some new treat. In one way she was a perfect match for him, since her moody silence gave Chester plenty of room to dream. But in another way she was a letdown, because she didn't offer the sort of commentary through which he could acquire an inspiration for his next move against the Wilsons.

Because of Lindy's limitations, therefore, Chester began hungering for a true confidant in crime, someone who might offer advice as he sketched his remaining options. This need, as well as the necessity of disproving the brothers' claim that they did not own the eighty acres, combined to persuade him at last that he must travel into Hickman and confront Selkirk. Why had the preacher disappeared for so many weeks when Chester required a go-between with Bill Beagle?

It might sound surprising that Chester had not sought out Selkirk earlier. Indeed, he had thought of him pretty often as the desperate spring days passed, but after all, Chester's opportunities for hitching a ride into town on Alistair's wagon were rare and the brothers were watching him closely, so he couldn't simply disappear for an afternoon without being questioned. Furthermore, though Chester had taken up churchgoing again, Selkirk refused to acknowledge his signals during the services. So finally Chester was driven to the extreme of slipping away from Alistair's place after dark and traversing the five miles to the parsonage on foot. When he arrived, Selkirk was out, so he had to wait until nearly midnight in his muddy pants and boots, when the preacher returned at last from his comfortable evening with the piano player. But when Selkirk saw Chester lurking in the shadows, he screamed, "O holy of holies!" and nearly bolted in terror. He had not consulted Bill Beagle about drawing up any papers, and he thought Chester might be carrying a stick or even a knife.

When Chester ran up and laid a hand on the preacher's arm and cried, "I got her! I got her stashed away!" Selkirk looked even more appalled. He had noticed Lindy missing from Sunday worship, but until that night he had fostered the hope that the girl was only seriously ill. If there'd been a kidnapping, he had reasoned, Chester would surely not be accompanying the family to church every week, as though he was still on the same terms with them as before. Selkirk found it incredible that the hired man had gone undetected for so long. Moreover, he was amazed that the Wilsons had kept the matter quiet; surely, Selkirk thought, if Chester had actually made an attempt on the girl, word would have spread quickly. Thus the news about Chester's bold, daring, dangerous, exciting, and bracing act, so far safely accomplished and awaiting only its big payoff, confounded all Selkirk's expectations and sent his head spinning. The preacher lapsed into extended ejaculations of surprise: "Why, praise the Lord for a turnip, that's impossible!" and the like. But eventually he was brought to an absolute belief in Chester's highly circumstantial and passionate story.

What Chester found most gratifying was that Selkirk's astonishment evolved into a mounting enthusiasm for the project. Selkirk offered a perspective which the kidnapper, enmeshed in day-to-day operations, had lost sight of. As the preacher pointed out, "If you've survived this long, why, that's a triumph in itself! If the whole business collapses tomorrow, you've still made your mark. Those mighty Wilsons have been forced to answer your notes. That cussed Alistair's been humbled into climbing a ladder and tying a cloth around a lightning rod. All the family routines have been shot to hell. Isn't that power? And you still got the girl. So you might even get some ransom pretty soon." For twenty or thirty minutes Selkirk's pulse beat faster and he forgot that Chester was a gap-toothed, filthy madman. He invited him inside the parsonage for a slug of whiskey. As usual around our country, when somebody fell into an enthusiastic fit, the course of events veered decisively.

Selkirk cheered up Chester enormously, giving him the strength to see the business through for a couple more weeks. Before their conversation, Chester had been thinking in his more desperate moments that it was not too late for him to escape to the train station some night and disappear. Now he grinned and grinned as he understood from the preacher that so far he had held the Wilsons to a draw.

By the time Chester struck out for Alistair's in the early morning darkness, Selkirk had broken his private vow and promised, "I'll go see the lawyer tomorrow about preparing those papers. You can count on that for Gospel now!"

"If you'd asked me that night," Chester said years afterward, "I'd have said I had it all in the bag. I could have kissed a grizzly bear, I was dancing and capering about so. Mud nor chill winds nor tiredness didn't matter to me then, no sir! Everything felt so *right!*"

Chapter Seven

As the earliest weeks of spring rolled by, she never felt restless, locked up in the familiar room. Chester had brought her a corncob doll of his own making, and if you've ever seen the old dilapidated tumbledown house where the girl was kept, you'll find yourself dreaming of the secrets she must have told that dolly in the long afternoons.

"All those spider webs up in the corners, Ma couldn't ever have allowed that when she lived here. She'd say, 'Lindy, you fetch that broom right now.' Funny, her sweeping the crumbs up every night, when we didn't even have furniture for some of the rooms nor separate beds for all us kids. Not having anything just made her all the cleaner. Held her back straight no matter how sick she felt. She'd lay in bed nights, moaning because her bones ached from the lifting and hauling she'd done all day. You'd think a person would let down with that much pain, and with Pa not able to make a go of the farm, so that some weeks he and Ma had to take turns skipping breakfast because there wasn't enough mush to go around. But no sir, she'd say, 'Come here with that broom, Lindy girl, there's cobwebs all over this parlor'— when I could only see one little strand way up there out of reach.

"Said she was going to take me to the doctor when times got better, because I moved so slow. Afraid my bones were brittle like hers, that they'd ache all my life from any little piece of work and nothing could cure it later on. But the times never turned while she was here, and now when we got the rain back, and crop prices are up, where is she, to do like she said?

"Of course the reason I moved so slow wasn't entirely the ache, like Ma thought. Truth is, there just wasn't much reason to hurry up. She and Pa'd been hurrying all their lives, and what'd it get them except more worry?

"The day Ma called me into the kitchen to tell me we were giving up farming and loading old Betsy for California, I was gladder than a prize hen. Get away from that bunch of snot-noses at the school, see some of the world for a change. Those little Hickman girls showed up every day with ribbons in their hair, pink or green or yellow, all except me and a couple of other kids, and they made us stay to one side of the playground while they pranced around playing hopscotch. Laughed at us because our homework was handed in on dirty paper, or because there was nothing between my bread for a sandwich at lunch.

"Once they yelled I had lice. That was a dirty lie! That other trashy girl, Brenda, she got lice three or four times, but never me. Not with my ma looking me over. She wouldn't have let a lice bug get into this house to save its soul. Except little Sharon caught it once and Ma had to scrub and pick her over for a few days. But still that wasn't me, was it? They were just yelling because they could, and I was poor so everybody believed them.

"Made me feel all sweaty in class because those teachers thought I was so stupid I couldn't remember the figures from yesterday on the blackboard. That old Miz Bazoom, she thought I couldn't even find my place in the reader without her leaning over and swiping my cheek with her chest while she turned the pages for me. Always made me sit in the back corner away from the windows, trying to keep me out of sight. Had to perch there and smell the schoolroom stink those boys were putting off till I just about gagged.

"So I was danged glad to be told we were getting out of

this place. Cold in the winter, muggy in the summer, and no-body much ever drove by our road that you could look at, except those Wilsons that never gave us the time of day. Ma was glad too, when she told me that.

"Then two nights later we held our arms round each other, hugging and crying, after Pa told Ma that I wasn't coming along. 'Why not?' she shouted at him. "Isn't she our own flesh and blood, just like the little ones? You think we can throw her off like a used-up dishrag?'

"Pa was looking out the back door into the yard. Finally he says, 'We needed the car engine overhauled, didn't we? And some cash to buy gas on the way out, didn't we? Can't go floating to California on a flying carpet, by God! So what choice did I have? It was the only deal I could make. These broken-down chairs are hardly worth six bits altogether, and Alistair wouldn't take the land unless I threw her in.'

"'Then none of us'll go,' says Ma. 'I won't sell my prettiest girl to be a slave to folks like that.'

"Pa just worked his mouth awhile, with her weeping at the table and me looking at him from behind, trying to see into his skull. Finally he says, 'Then we'll all starve together. You want that?'

"'No,' says Ma real low.

"That week we hadn't had anything but potatoes and a little pork fat to eat. All the canned string beans were gone by then.

"Pa says, 'If she doesn't work out up at Alistair's, they'll pass her down the road till one of the families suits her.'

"'How'll she find us again when her two years are up?' says Ma.

"'You'll write back to her when we get us a settled place and can afford to pay her way out,' he says.

"No letter's come yet, though. Unless Mister Alistair just tore it up, once he saw I could haul buckets and the little ones would mind me.

"Really, I didn't care so much about not going to California once I found out I was going to work at the Wilsons, though. Cousin Sophie always dressed nice for church, and all the little kids looked smart and clean when they came to school. Never had been inside their house before, but somebody said they had soft padded chairs and a braided rug on the parlor floor. I wasn't going to be trash any longer, I'd go back to that school wearing a clean dress every day.

"That's what I thought before I moved. Never figured they wouldn't send me back to school, just keep me in the house to help Cousin Sophie all day. Mister Alistair said I read and cyphered good enough for a girl already, which was true enough, what'd I want to read any more books for? But still, I bet Ma would've been awfully surprised.

"When I saw what kind of slave they were making of me, I just slowed down like I had before, when I lived in this house. What's the reason for bustling around when you're just making somebody else richer, not your own self? Never got a new dress, except one of Cousin Sophie's hand-me-downs for church, and went barefoot half the summer before anybody noticed I could use some new shoes. At least I'm eating regular now, which is a nice change, though the way that family hogs it down does make me sick to watch them.

"The Wilson women are nothing like Ma. Is that because they're rich, I wonder, or were they raised shrewish, or is it because of the way their husbands treat them? Ma could be short-tempered with me too, but that was only because she had so many calls on her time. I never blamed her too much. First time I got the curse, that was a hard night. Johnny and Mae both had the chickenpox and Ma was nursing them the best she could, running downstairs every once in a while to cook for the rest of us. And there I was with the blood staining my drawers and I didn't even know where it'd come from. Could have been dying, for all I knew. Sure as heck thought I was worse off than those kids with the chickenpox.

But she just tossed me a rag, said, 'Here, you'll have to learn how to mop yourself up, I haven't got the time.' I couldn't sleep a wink that night, I was so scared in my gut. Hard to forgive her for not showing me how to keep the rag between my legs, but still, you just mainly felt sorry for her.

"But now you take those Wilson women. Only thing that holds them back is, they're afraid of one another's tongues, and of how their menfolks might cuff them if they said everything on their minds. Oh, they're real polite, 'Hello sister,' 'Why hello you're looking peachy today sister,' 'Why thank you my dear.' But then you just look at how Cousin Vera and Cousin Liza treated Cousin Sophie after they got the excuse of her being caught with that preacher—which every one of them would have offered her right arm for the chance of. They gave her a tongue-lashing about your sluts and your whores and what if we were to tell our dead pappy on you, till she was weeping and begging them for mercy, and then they huffed out, grinning to each other on the sly over how they'd taken her down. I had to pick Cousin Sophie up and put her to bed after they drove off, she was so wrung out. Give them half a reason, they jump on each other like cats in a barrel.

"And what kind of mothers they are! Little Kermit comes to me for a story or when somebody beats him up, before he'll go to his own ma. Bet she doesn't even notice the way he's afraid of her. If one of those kids gets a knock on the noggin, he'd best not cry out, because she'll thump him another one and tell him to shut up. If she would've run off with that preacher, I bet not one of those kids would've cried a tear. Well, that didn't work out though, did it? I thought as soon as old Stringbean proposed his crazy scheme that it sounded too good to be true. Imagine believing he could bring off such a trick.

"I've watched the Wilson men with their wives plenty of times. They wouldn't dare pinch a fanny if they were alone with one of the women—they only do it if another man's standing close by to share the joke. 'Hello, Miz Baby-Maker,' they say, and the wife says, "Stuff and nonsense, I'll baby-maker you,' and those men hightail it out of the kitchen together chuckling to beat the band.

"Lordy, it's just there for the tasting, if the men weren't so shy. You don't catch livestock treating it like it was some big secret. So why the men? But anyway, it's no wonder all the Wilson women want to escape. Who wouldn't, if they were married to lummoxes like that? One thing about the preacher, he knew what to do when he was alone with a gal in the parlor. Or it looked like he did for a while, before he chickened out.

"If only I wasn't stuck in the middle of nowhere, with all the boys thinking I was trash, then I'd whip into action myself. Nothing to it for a gal, if you can just keep a straight face when they come up and whisper how they're about to die for you. Out in California I would've had a good chance to get a couple of fellas for myself out of all those strangers, once I got away from Pa and Ma.

"Question is, would I really want to make up to any man like I've seen so far? You can cuss them so they'll shy from you in the daylight, but at night they'll throw you around like a feed sack and not much you can do. Look at me, I ended up dumped in a cold empty farmhouse with no one to talk to but Stringbean and this old dolly, all because I shut my eyes a minute when he came for me, thinking I was about to be loved."

"Lying here all night in the cold, can hardly feel my fingers, my toes are far away as the stars. I'm all drawn up inside my head, behind my eyes. I look into the dark, I see things you can't see in the day.

"I remember when the Depression came, that's when Ma started moaning about the baby not getting enough to eat.

'These are the worst times ever known to the human race,' and on and on. But finally she just shut up. Nothing changed, only she got distracted by other things and figured the Depression was living too, once you got used to the feel of it.

"Pa was the one who never adjusted. Kept saying, 'Oh it's all my fault.' Then he'd change his face and say, 'Oh how do they expect a man to feed his family in such hard times when they've gone and wrecked the whole country?' Then again he'd take up with, 'Oh it's all my own fault anyway.' He was just stumbling around like that, about to lose his head, ever since I knew him.

"You can look at the way those Wilsons manage and see what went wrong for Pa. Nothing in the bank, nothing in the barn, nobody to fall back on, except his children that mostly weren't old enough to work. When the going's tough, you got to have something strong to buck you up, like your brothers, or maybe if you're a derned sight cleverer than Pa you can get by on your own . . .

"Blessed is the weak, I can't see why they say that. In the end Pa was just as mean to me as anybody with a backbone could have been. Lordy, if you think about it, he sold me for a little travel money. Even the Wilsons wouldn't have done that to their own daughter, say what you like about them.

"Don't care if I never run into Pa out in California. What are we going to say to one another after all this? 'Good morning, Pa, that couldn't keep his family together,' and then, 'Good morning, Lindy Sue, are you still a virgin or did you trade that away too? Hope at least you made a good bargain for it.' So I says, 'If you think you're getting half, you got another think coming, so put your stinking hand back in your pocket!"

"Now even old Chester gets into the act, hoping he can make two bits out of my hide. Everybody's trading off me, passing me around to see what the next fellow'll pay. Seems about time I kept a little profit for myself.

"Being kidnapped can be a pretty good life, though, if you got a bozo like him to fetch for you. Except blankets—you'd think if he planned this business so good, he'd have found some way to snitch a couple more. Afraid my danged toes are going to fall off one of these nights if warm weather doesn't come pretty quick. Can't tell if that black stuff around the nails is just dirt or something worse, like when a potato freezes. Better not worry about that or the night'll be past before I can settle my brain down again."

When Selkirk sidled into Bill Beagle's office to ask a few questions about conveying a land title, the lawyer pricked up his ears. He remembered his odd interview with Chester months before, and he knew at once the piece of land in question. When Beagle wanted to learn something that might prove amusing, he was enormously patient. Little by little he extracted nearly the whole tale of the kidnapping from the preacher, who had planned to preserve an entirely theoretical frame of reference. At last Beagle cut through Selkirk's remaining defenses. "You mean that blamed hired man's gone and snatched her, don't you?"

When Selkirk allowed, in a frightened voice, that you might put it that way if you were so inclined, Beagle snapped back, "Then what we're dealing with's a capital offense! I won't have anything to do with it till the girl's brought home. Now I got some advice for you, first as a lawyer and next as one professional man speaking to another. If you aid or abet a criminal, you can be sent to the pen right along with the guy that did it. Safest thing is for you to call at the sheriff's office and unload your conscience. That's my legal counsel. Number two, you got to start thinking more about your position. You're a minister of the Gospel. What're you running around talking to such riffraff for? Don't you know enough to keep your nose clean? Why, if that hired man tried to pull me into the gutter, I'd shout him down like thunder!"

By the time Selkirk backed out of Beagle's office, he must have looked badly frazzled. After those words about aiding and abetting, he would naturally have seen Chester in a harsher light. His previous fears now redoubled; he wondered if he'd already waded too deep in sin, and he lacked the nerve to seek out the sheriff and report what he knew. I can imagine him slinking back to the parsonage and writhing in a kind of apprehensive torment which was as close as he ever came to prayer.

Beagle didn't report Selkirk's story to the sheriff either. For one thing, he didn't know how much to believe. He wasn't sure whether the snatch had actually occurred, or whether Chester and Selkirk were merely trying to find out if such a scheme would be worth their effort. He was also enough of a country lawyer to know the difference between a practical joke and a crime worth prosecuting. He detected the comic small potatoes aspect of this kidnapping from the fear he saw twisted on Selkirk's face. After the preacher left, he fell into a cascade of chuckles, dripping cigar ashes down his vest and scattering them over the papers stacked before him. That evening he recounted the whole interview to his poker-playing cronies, including the other lawyer who practiced in Hickman, a couple of bankers, and old Stewart, the editor of the Hickman *Sun*. That's why, within forty-eight hours after Chester paid Selkirk a visit by night, there was a reporter driving through the thick mud to Alistair's house, instructed to inquire about Miss Lindy Douglas, rumored missing.

The reporter, Johnny Acorn, was called from Hickman by the war, so like my Uncle Donny and my Cousin Lindy, I know him only by reputation. Still, many points are clear enough. He started out as a cub reporter on the Kansas City *Star*, but was soon let go because of hard times. But by then newspapers were in his blood, so he cast about for another reporting job, and after many futile applications he finally settled for the *Sun*. In those days our local paper was still run by its founder, old man Stewart, and—except for the printer—Johnny Acorn was his only employee: assistant editor, secretary, subscription agent, copyboy. Twice a week they produced an eight-page tabloid recording the local illnesses and church socials and livestock market reports. The *Sun* almost never found any hard news to print. Generally, Johnny Acorn did his reporting by sitting at the phone and jotting down the names and dates called in by housewives and club leaders. The *Sun* never printed pictures: the press wasn't set up for them, and neither Stewart nor Johnny owned a camera.

Johnny's story, like Chester's, holds my attention mainly because he was another irrepressible idealist to whom the obvious impediments did not appear obvious. He was fascinated by the romance of the press, inspired by having rubbed shoulders with the vigorous K.C. reporters, and fired by the righteous indignation of some muckraking novels that fell into his hands. He left a complete set of Upton Sinclair at his rooming house when he went into the Navy. He must have realized the Hickman *Sun* wasn't very close to real journalism, but he could get no nearer to it for the time being, and he evidently fancied that if he hung on until conditions improved, his faithfulness to the profession might be rewarded by a post on some bigger masthead. Those who remembered him said that he lived by a kind of dogged hopefulness all through the decade and reached his early thirties without marrying any of the local girls. His spirit was too agitated by the fumes of newsprint and social causes (which he perhaps only partly understood, stuck off in the boonies while Chicago and California festered). If he cherished any great wish, it must have been that some story worth reporting, full of social significance and drama, might carry his by-line all over the Midwest, "courtesy the Hickman *Sun*." Probably he kept his pencil sharpened and saved a few pages at the back of his notebook in readiness for the news to break. Given that Hickman is located squarely in a region of near misses, he almost got his desire.

Johnny stood as tall as Chester and appeared almost as thin, though he dressed like a city fellow and spoke better. When he knocked at Alistair's front door the first time, Sophie peered through the curtains for five minutes before she answered suspiciously. Later she claimed not to have told the stranger anything; she denied having heard of Lindy, then asserted that the girl didn't live with them anymore, and when Johnny, who was beginning to wonder at such defensiveness, asked her bluntly, "There been a snatch around here?" Sophie slammed the door in his face. The Wilsons didn't hold her responsible for giving out information—no wife on our road would have done that—but they blamed her for failing to lie convincingly enough. Because Johnny certainly did not go away. When Alistair came up to the house for dinner, the reporter met him at the back gate.

Alistair greeted any stranger warily until he'd discovered if there was some possibility of gain. But when Johnny asked about Lindy, my uncle's eyes narrowed and he said, "You representing her family?"

Possibly it crossed Johnny's mind to allege that he was, and see what information that duplicity might win him. But if so, he brushed the temptation aside, for he was eager to say the words, "Nope, I'm a reporter for the Hickman *Sun!*"

Alistair had never been so stunned. The full meaning of a visit from a newspaperman was beyond his comprehension at that moment—he had no idea how the story about Lindy had gotten out, no idea if a reporter in his backyard might lead to worse interference by outsiders, no conception of whether or not it was possible to win an advantage from a fellow like Johnny. All the possibilities would have to be talked out privately with his brothers. In the meantime, Alistair acted on his instincts as a farmer and a Wilson.

"You see that mailbox at the road?" he pointed. Johnny

nodded. "When you're on this side of that mailbox, you're trespassing. When you're on the other side, you're OK in the sight of the law and the good Lord."

Both men took a good last look at one another, then Johnny got in his car and backed down to the road. He turned in the direction of town, pulled up fifty feet, and killed the engine. A moment later, to Alistair's annoyance, he took out a lunch sack and started eating a sandwich. When Alistair looked through the parlor window again after his own dinner, he saw that Johnny had finished his meal and was reading a book propped against the steering wheel. Alistair was afraid to drive down to consult with his brothers about this new complication, because he'd have to pass the reporter's car. Besides, he feared what that snoop might get into while he was away.

Late in the afternoon Chester noticed the strange parked vehicle. Johnny had gotten out to pee, and the movement attracted Chester's eyes to that spot on the horizon. He asked Alistair who the fellow was. Alistair was peeved enough to feel in an experimental mood, so he held nothing back. "Says he's a reporter. Come asking about Lindy."

Chester's eyes bugged, and his silence gave off the smell of panic. Alistair saw he hadn't thrown this information away for nothing—it suddenly became clear to him that if he was upset by the reporter, Chester must be twice as nervous. Because once outsiders started meddling, it wouldn't matter how much Chester protested that he was the underdog and righteous hero of the affair. In any official version, the Wilsons were going to be called the patient sufferers, the aggrieved relatives who were being tortured by a mad inhuman dog of a kidnapper.

Johnny Acorn spent most of two weeks casing one Wilson farm or another. He asked the children questions on their way home from school. He tramped over the surrounding fields on days when the clouds lifted long enough for the grass to dry. Once he noticed a hired hand working at Alistair's, he set out to seduce Chester to the far side of the mailbox for interrogation. This took awhile because of Chester's fears, but finally Johnny called out, "Want a smoke?" so Chester decided it would look suspicious if he refused.

Alistair had given no orders about whether or not Chester should talk. In fact, once Johnny appeared, everybody on our road—roused by their new belief in Chester's ability to generate a story—shared the feeling that this unexpected ingredient might be sufficient to push the hired hand toward his inevitable climax, so they all resolved to keep hands off and let Chester hang himself if he would. Sophie only peered through the parlor window every time she heard the reporter shouting to Chester, and took careful note of the two men's expressions as they smoked together. She saw the reporter talk a blue streak and point in various directions around the countryside, though Chester never let out more than two or three words which, from the shaking of his head, must have expressed his violent denials.

Seeing that Chester was vulnerable to the temptation of free tobacco, Johnny drove back once or twice in the evening and brought along a couple of cigars for extra persuasion. The two men sat together on the running board in the chilly April evenings, Johnny asking all sorts of questions about farm life, such as what Chester was paid for his labor and how many hours he worked and what sort of life Alistair's family pursued. Occasionally he blended in some question about Lindy—about her appearance, her moods, the likelihood that she had simply run away. But quite apart from these newsworthy subjects, Johnny was mainly thinking, no doubt, as he and Chester drew smoke through their stogies, of how similar (and proletarian) their tastes were, despite all their apparent differences of status and education.

Chester didn't know what to make of Johnny's inquisitiveness, yet he was unable to tear himself away. He was partly fascinated, as a chicken may be charmed by a snake. Sometimes he could tell what the reporter was getting at, and then he answered on principle with a deliberate lie; but other times he didn't know whether to tell a tall one or the truth. When Johnny inquired about his wages, was he trying to find out if Chester had an economic motive for kidnapping somebody, or was he just passing the time? So Chester lied once, then backtracked when a similar question came up later, and finally couldn't remember what story he'd told. The reporter kept him in a tizzy, nearly boxing him in a corner more than once. Besides, Chester was prevented from seeing Lindy sometimes when Johnny wouldn't let him go for two hours, plying him with smoke after smoke. And what was Chester living for, moment by moment, if not to snatch the opportunity when he could to sneak over the hill and gaze at her, talk to her, for a desperate, joyous half hour? Johnny's attentions thus provided one more pressure, when Chester already felt so distracted that he thought he couldn't stand any more. Where was that preacher with the legal papers? It was time to get this business over with!

All Chester's apprehensions appear ironic to me, because once, during an Easter vacation from college, I spent some hours looking up the couple of articles Johnny Acorn wrote for the *Sun* during the period when he was persecuting the hired man with those questions. I had some half-baked idea that I might be able to use the old stories for a project in a journalism class I was taking, though they turned out to be quite different from what I'd expected. Anyway, I carried one of them home and showed it—four paragraphs entitled "Portrait of a Rural Hired Hand"—to Chester. At first he chuckled in recognition at the details from his own earlier life, but he ended in a rage over finding himself described as a "farm laborer with a pathetic stammer, the victim of poor nutrition that has dulled his faculties and left him incapable of answering even the simplest questions."

The other story Johnny wrote about his early observations of our territory, by the way, was not about Chester at all, but had genuine news value—though again it bore witness to the reporter's agitated social conscience. A gang of "aimless rural youths" had been spotted wandering over the countryside. "They appear sullen and alienated. The desperate farm economy holds no place or hope for them: consequently they squander their time searching for objects to destroy and people to frighten. Their slouching forms," Johnny wrote, "testify to the social disintegration that results from hard times." The only person to observe Donny's decline carefully and lament it unselfishly was this newspaperman, who

Now, if Chester couldn't fathom all that lay beneath Johnny's questions, nevertheless the reporter's repeated visits did at last push him beyond patience with Selkirk, who had never appeared with the legal papers as promised. On the evening of May 2, when Johnny started up his engine to drive into town for supper, Chester asked, "Mind if I ride along?" He didn't pause to tell anybody where he was headed, so as Alistair stared after the car, he wondered if he would ever see his tom-fool hired man again. He also wondered if his brothers would blame him for not trying to prevent the escape. But the family had agreed to give Chester free rein, and this was simply one of the risks they had to accept. Alistair realized that if Chester never came back, then Lindy was possibly lost, and they had been fools for not apprehending him when they could. All the brothers tossed and sweated a good bit about Chester's disappearance before morning.

Meanwhile, Johnny let Chester out in front of the Lassos' hotel. Chester didn't bother to dodge and weave in order to throw the reporter off his trail, though it seems that Johnny did not follow. But Chester's boldness gives some idea of how strongly resolved he was. "Figured maybe that'd been my trouble—hadn't stomped my foot and insisted we get this show on the road. I'd been begging and bellyaching, letting those Wilsons put me off and taking the preacher's word, when he'd always proved undependable. So I just marched into that lawyer's office—he was closing up for supper—and I says, 'How about it?' He knew what I was talking about, oh yes! Didn't have to ask me more than two questions till he figured out the whole story. That proves what a common-sense idea it was, if a smart fellow like him could see so quick how it would work. He knew it was only natural to snatch Miss Lindy and if you were going to do that, the only thing to ask for was those eighty acres. No farmer in those days had cash, all they owned was land and livestock, and how could I get out of town with a bunch of sheep under my coat? So it had to be land, and when I told him I needed some proof of who owned the property and some papers to be signed, he said, 'No trouble at all. Just have to look up the title in the courthouse and have my secretary type the form. Take about three days.' When two men that know the world get down to business, you can settle something in two shakes.

"I asked him, 'How'm I going to get those papers?' and he says, 'The preacher'll bring them out.' But I told him, 'Selkirk's let me down once too often to be trusted.' He chuckled, because he knew the character we were dealing with, but all the same he says, 'I'll talk to him, and he'll do it.' I was feeling pretty confident, so I says, 'Lawyer Beagle, anything you guarantee, it's okeydoke by me.' We shook hands and I walked the five miles back to Alistair's to wait. He showed he was a gentleman by not pressing me about a fee. He trusted that if I turned a profit, I'd remember him. And if I didn't turn a profit, that was one of the risks of his trade. I took my time walking home, knowing the boss'd be wondering if I was ever coming back. All the way I was thinking, if Beagle believes in me enough to do me favors, things'll start falling in my lap right quick. I felt like I was sitting pretty that night, even more than the night I'd talked to the preacher last."

Alistair too must have felt great forces moving when he saw Chester step out of his cabin for the milking next morning as usual. He figured his hired man had gone into town to arrange something critical, possibly under pressure from the reporter's questions or even—who knows?—with the reporter's connivance. It was time to find out what was cooking. So Alistair made a snap decision without consulting his brothers, trusting to the Wilson gab and to the magic of events. Right after breakfast he wrote a note and gave it to Chester, telling him to post it for the kidnapper. When Chester unfolded the paper down in his cabin, he read, "Stop killing my chickens you win. I'll meet wherever you say. Bring any paper you want me to sign, also proof the girl is OK." You can imagine that as Chester read this unexpected message of surrender, Alistair was nervously pacing about the barn, wondering if there was any way in God's green earth for his hired man to escape from the trap he had concocted.

Chapter Eight

All the time Chester thought he was drawing closer to his goal with the Wilsons, Lindy seems to have suspected that things were sliding from bad to worse. Toward the end, she grew restless as a cat and started making her own plans.

"Now, what do you make of that? First I hear him unbolting the door as usual, so I waltz over, thinking maybe I'll weasel something out of him with a big juicy kiss on the mouth, but this time when he sees me coming he throws up his arms like to hit me in the jaw, and he says, 'I've taken enough off of you! You're a demon-witch just like all the rest of those Wilson women!'

"I back off and say, 'What do you mean? My name isn't Wilson.'

"He says, 'No, but you're worse than they are, anyway. You think you're Miss Hoity-Toity because you carry slop for the big house. You came down to my cabin when I was fixing things up for your lady to escape with the preacher, and instead of thanking me kindly, you drop threats like I was a dog to be whipped.'

"'She made me say those things because she was so nervous,' I say.

"He says, 'Then when the preacher ran off without her, which I couldn't help, you rubbed my nose in it just like you were her. You fixed up those dinners for me with carpet tacks in the mashed potatoes—'

"'We didn't ever use carpet tacks! Besides, those things

were just a little joke that she did all by herself, after I'd dished up your plate and it was sitting on the counter waiting to be taken down to you.'

"'In a pig's eye,' he says. 'And then, because you found out you couldn't choke me or poison me, you called in that Donny-boy and pushed him into picking a fight with me—'

"'Now, that's just a danged lie. I never called him down at all. I didn't even like the looks of him, wasting the air he took up with his sighs, when somebody else could have used it. Besides, what do you think the family would have done to me if I'd let on like I was going after him? Every time he came to gawk at me, Cousin Sophie'd pinch me black and blue and tell me to stop whoring with my eyes, or else I'd be out in the road for good with no dinners. So he wasn't doing me any favors by coming around, was he?

"'Then finally when I never gave him any encouragement, he sort of popped—got it into his head that I liked you better than him for some reason. I don't know how.'

"Old Stringbean was quiet for a minute, pulling on his chin. At last he says, 'A man doesn't know what to believe. Everybody around here's got a silver tongue that can lead you astray.'

"'Those others tell lies,' I say, 'but not me. I know better.'

"'Not even about liking me better than Donny?'

"'I didn't say that, I said that's what he thought.'

"'Then what's the truth? Who do you like, besides yourself?'

"'What'd you come out here for anyway? You brought me more wood, or that coat I asked for, or those slippers? Or are you just here to yell at me for things I couldn't help?'

"'I came to tell you you build a man up and then when he thinks he's as high as he can go, you turn away and down he falls. I came out to tell you I got you whether you like it or not, and if you try to escape, I'll bust your fanny.'

"'I don't need any busting,' I say, 'nor any men to raise their voices at me. I haven't tried to get away yet, but when I want to, I will, so you can just go back where you came from and stew in your own juice.'

"'You may not need me,' he says, 'but I got you, and I'm going to keep you, and when they finally turn over the property, I'm going to fling you in their faces like a worn-out dishrag!' And he stomps out and bolts the door again before I could answer him one more.

"But good lord! What's he want from me? I didn't ask to be kidnapped, did I? Nor I don't ask him to come out here at all to visit me, if he's going to act like that. It was nice when he was shy and slow, those first couple of weeks after he'd snatched me, but now his mind's turned somehow. If he gets any wilder, I'm just pulling up one of these windows and slipping back to Cousin Sophie's on my own, snatch or no snatch. That was a good joke in the beginning, I was glad to get a rest, but who's laughing now? Nobody, that's who."

"WHEN old Stringbean first showed up looking for that stupid goat, he had the newest face I'd ever seen. Didn't even dare look straight at him for a couple of weeks, he seemed so strange. Oh, he was dirty all right, you could see he was hungry as a bear and smell him coming a mile off. Still, something about him grabbed me. He acted like the road. He had foreign ways, how he held his bread over his plate when he ate, like as if to guard his food, like something might happen to it if he didn't. It made you think, where's he been that he had to learn that?

"Now I see he isn't so special. Surprised he's even got the brains left to think up this stupid idea. Kidnapping me, isn't that nuts! What he should have done was kept on traveling, instead of stopping here in this lonesome country. That's what I'll do. See it all once I get out of this old house. No use going back to Cousin Sophie's and lug water buckets all my life!

"Reminds me how Pa used to drive us to Hickman in the wagon, and once three years ago we borrowed a truck and drove into Saint Joe itself. Saw the stockyards, everyplace crawling with flies, and the smell! Thought I'd die. Eating houses up and down the street right across from the packing plants. They all had signs like 'Best steak in the world,' but who could chew it, when all you could think about was those cows bawling in those filthy holding pens?

"But what really took my breath is how many folks you could see in a big place like that, and every face different. Even in Hickman, whenever you drive in, twenty faces you never saw before. Makes you wonder that there could be so many noses, so many different ears.

"That's what you'd see if you traveled all around, to California or down to K.C. You'd see how different everything could get. All the nice things come from someplace else anyway. Like cars, and Cousin Sophie's sewing machine. They're never just sitting here at home, you got to go out and find them. Imagine wanting to settle down, for goodness' sake! Never sticking your head up and seeing what's over the next hill, like these Wilsons that just sit on the same property year after year, watching their crops come up. Bet their kids won't stick around, any more than I'm going to. But maybe they will, they're Wilsons, they'll own it all someday. That makes a difference."

"WELL, he was gentler this evening at least. 'Come back to apologize,' he says. 'Sorry I lost my temper, but when I look at you, sometimes I can't stand to think about that Donny, or about those nasty words you spoke to me—'

"'What I said, I had to say. Fact that you're disappointed doesn't give you any right to haul me out here without asking if I want to come, nor to make money off me by holding me here. Now if we were to split it, that'd be different.'

"'Split it?' he says. Then he backs against the door and slides onto the floor, slow, like he was thinking all the way down. He just looks straight at his shoe for minute after minute, till I thought he'd fallen into a fit. Had a stroke or something. Then he looks up, fixes me with those saucer eyes, tells me, 'You want to split it, okeydoke. I'll split it with my wife.'

"Now, how'm I supposed to answer that? I say, 'A gal's got to think these things over mighty careful. How would we live? Where would we go?'

"'Live like a princess if you wanted,' he says. 'Wouldn't have to go anywhere. Money'll start rolling in just as soon as I get what I want out of those Wilsons. Then you can have clothes as pretty as your face, and I'll never raise a hand against you.'

"Like a princess! I thought. After that I treated him real kindly, told him we'd talk more about it later. Maybe I could get some of his profit out of him by saying I'd marry, and then I wouldn't have to hitch, I could buy me a train ticket anywhere I wanted, just like the big swells.

"*If* he makes them pay any ransom, that is. Chances are hard to figure at this point. Those Wilsons couldn't care enough to give much for me, but then I never thought they'd let him walk around free for so many days, so maybe there's things afoot I don't know about. Maybe he's so crazy-smart he's got them buffaloed, and they'll pay up just to see what he'll do next."

"THAT old Tiger had the greenest eyes. Pa said she was a tramp, of course, because she'd go off for a couple days and creep around spitting at the tomcats. Brought home that rat's tail in her mouth one time—ugh! she was a bloody mess.

Must've rolled in the carcass after she'd killed it. Wouldn't let us near her with a water bucket. Licked herself clean in the yard, one stroke at a time with her little pink tongue, swallowing all that gore inside her. Kept the rat tail someplace—up a tree probably—then every day or two you'd see her worrying it in the yard, shake shake, like it was some toy. Finally fell apart on her, one bone at a time just broke off. Don't know if cats bury things like that, or if she let them drop where they fell.

"But you could look in her eyes and she'd look right back, not blinking, like she knew just as much as you, only she wasn't telling, she was keeping it all for herself. Sometimes she wouldn't let you come close, but other days you could stroke her fur backwards if she was in the mood, and there under the orange stripes you'd find it was a whole different color: it was kind of light brown at first, then suddenly at the bottom it got real creamy, almost to white, and beneath that she was still keeping her actual skin a secret, because the hair was so thick.

"Now, that was a color like you don't see around much—nothing can match the colors on a real fine silky cat. That's why they lick themselves so much, they know it's special. They enjoy looking it over, all the little secret spots that only they know are there. When they go prowling around, like the yard was a jungle, they're thinking, 'Well mister, you can't see in my armpit, but I know what's there, and it's all beautiful golden-white cat hair, that a king would give his crown to grow on his head, but he can't. It's mine, I don't have to show it, I can just think about it any time I want. It's my treasure, my gold.'

"Probably run off when Pa and Ma left, and lives along the crick. Funny she didn't find me up at Cousin Sophie's and come mewing for a plate of milk. Better off on her own, though, where she can hunt field mice and the Wilson kids won't grab at her and stop her going where she pleases. Some animals need petting and some don't. Tiger'll get along okeydoke."

"Now they can just smash him to smithereens and I won't care a bit! They can cut open his white belly and gut him like he was a catfish! I never heard of such stupidness!

"If he'd come and told me what he was planning to do earlier, I could've steered him off that idea. Imagine, asking for a piece of property right under the Wilsons' noses for the ransom. And my Pappy's land to boot! 'You think I have to be kidnapped in order to live in this house where I was born?' I told him. Live like a princess, my foot! Nobody ever made that kind of money off these fields up till now. I'd like to see what kind of farming old Stringbean could do that'd turn this place into a gold mine!

"What's he want to hang around here for anyway? Let's get on the road! Ask for something that isn't nailed down! No wonder they're closing in on him—they know he's the only sap dumb enough to cook that one up. Some folks you just can't help, they got to go and jinx themselves. No sir, when they come and find me, if they ask any questions about old Sour-Face, I'll send him up the river in a minute. Doesn't do any good to stand by somebody without the brains of a gnat.

"Now he tells me there's a newspaperman snooping around at the Wilsons, standing out by the mailbox of an evening, poking into the barn, asking everybody questions. All that kind of nosing that they do. If the reporter's got half a mind, he'll walk out and look over this old house some morning and see me through a window. Then the game'll be up. You got to finish a business like this quick. Once they call in the reporters, your goose is cooked.

"Lordy, I hope that fella doesn't take my picture! Pop pop pop, that's all I'd need: plastered on the front pages everywhere, looking like a bug-eyed piece of white trash. Once that happens, there wouldn't be any use of hitting the road. Might as well give up the ghost, because folks'd know me wherever I went. Can't hope to rise once everybody sees that. This is just about the worst end a gal could think of. If you fall into the hands of a stupid ignoramus, you're going to get done in sure. I should've broken out of here that first night and gone back to bed like nothing happened. Or better yet, turned in old Sawdust-Brain to Mister Alistair. Then at least we'd have had quiet around here, I could've got on with my chores in peace. Isn't any way this business can end happy now."

After his interview with Chester, Bill Beagle passed the word to old Stewart that the kidnapping was about to break. Johnny Acorn, in turn, was instructed to lurk about Alistair's place by night and expect fireworks. Then Beagle called in the Reverend Selkirk and handed over a legal-sized document, full of "wherefores" and "party of the third parts," ending with a couple of blank lines on which the Wilsons and Chester could sign their names if they were so foolish. Selkirk was again amazed, because when he'd left Beagle's office the last time, he had been convinced of the lawyer's unshakable disapproval. What he saw now was apparently another miracle wrought by Chester, who must have succeeded in bringing Beagle around. Selkirk doubtless felt contrite: that simple, ugly hired hand now stood close to acquiring eighty fine acres and a vacant farmhouse, while he had held back, frozen by useless fears. So the preacher agreed to convey the document; and when the lawyer added with a wink, "I think old Chester might need you to hang around and give him some more help to bring off the signing" (a guess by Beagle, who had by now sniffed out the delicious possibilities of this story and wanted to plunge Selkirk up to his ears in the muck), the preacher was sufficiently impressed to agree that he'd do whatever Chester asked, now and forever.

The meeting between the kidnapper and Alistair was set for the night of May 5, a Thursday, at a point where the creek circles an outcropping of brush and crowded trees, just before it flows from Alistair's farm into the contested eighty acres. Lindy, who must have been nearly bored out of her mind by now and on the verge of escaping, was alerted to pack her few comforts in a gunnysack and be ready for delivery. Selkirk was stationed along the creek below the meeting place and instructed to watch for Alistair.

"If he comes alone, you hoot once like an owl," Chester told him. (The two of them practiced hooting and gradually evolved a passably authentic sound, though unfortunately for the plan, Chester could produce it more consistently than Selkirk; he had practiced it softly on that night when he sat guard by the elm stump in the drizzle.) "But if you see the brothers coming along with Alistair, or if you see he's carrying a club or a shotgun, for God's sake hoot three times, so I'll be able to make a run for it!"

To satisfy Alistair's questions, Chester had ready in his pocket a dated note from Lindy, describing the day's weather (showery in the morning but clearing by afternoon, leading to a moonlit night). He also carried some of her toenail parings which he had begged, though I believe he planned to keep these for his own solace.

Chester debated with himself whether to appear before Alistair in his own person or in disguise. He craved the satisfaction of forcing his boss to acknowledge who had outsmarted him, but he also feared that if Alistair was made to deal with a mere hired hand face-to-face, he might get on his high horse and refuse to sign the transfer papers. Better show up in some costume, Chester decided; there would be time afterward for revelation. So Chester confiscated three or four gunnysacks from Lindy's bed and stitched them together with twine, cut out armholes and a place for eyes, and crept down to the rendezvous looking like an old tree root.

He found a place to hide among other roots on the muddy bank and nervously waited for the hoot of an owl.

After half an hour he heard the rustling of human steps, and then Alistair's voice shouted, "Ho there, you!"

Could that stupid Selkirk have watched in the wrong direction, or had he hooted too faintly? Chester was furious that his security system had failed. As a precaution (though he knew it was pretty useless), he called out in the false bass voice he had decided to adopt, "You come alone?" Alistair affirmed that he had.

After Alistair recovered from his surprise at seeing a column of gunnysacks climb toward him from the creek, and Chester had peered around in the shadows as best he could through his tiny eye slits to determine that no other Wilsons lurked in the shadows, the kidnapper handed over the note from Lindy, the legal document to be signed, and a pencil. Alistair held the pieces of paper up to the moonlight for scrutiny a long while, then asked, "Where's the girl?"

Chester repeated their agreement. "After you sign this paper, you're supposed to wait on the spot and I'll bring her up within the hour."

But Alistair claimed a different understanding. "I thought we agreed the girl's supposed to be waiting right here where I can see she's alive. Otherwise what's to keep you from stealing away without us ever getting ahold of her again?"

Chester replied testily, "Handing over the ransom always works this way—you could read a hundred cases in the newspapers every day!"

Alistair asked, "When have you ever been able to afford a newspaper?"

After that, the two men quickly fell to wrangling, with charges of bad faith on both sides, and their voices rose from stealthy whispers to angry shouts and curses. It was like any afternoon when they worked side by side in the field—they couldn't resist contradicting one another, and Chester, who wanted the whole business finished immediately, had nearly reached the point of stamping his feet in frustration, when suddenly he realized that Alistair had stopped arguing and his face had warped into a broad grin. On three sides of the little promontory where they stood, Chester now heard the rustling of more human feet. All at once he saw that he had been trapped. Selkirk was no doubt tied and gagged somewhere beneath the moon, and the jig was nearly up. Chester growled fiercely and almost jumped at Alistair's throat, but he caught himself in time, understanding how futile the struggle would be, one against four. Then he bolted.

His gunnysack legs slowed him down badly and he couldn't see much through the holes in his headpiece, so it seemed a miracle when he eluded all the brothers and ran freely into the eighty acres. Though he still heard rustling behind him, his pursuers never grew closer. Thus Chester was able to settle into an even stride and plan where he would try to hide. He thought that if he could slip to the far side of the hedgerow that came down to the creek, he would be protected by shadows until he reached the house where Lindy was waiting. He might lose the Wilsons before they got to the house and slip inside unnoticed, since they seemed to be coming on so slowly; or if they were still on his tail, he might lock the door against them and see what hiding places the basement or attic offered.

Actually, there was no reason for him to worry about reaching the old farmhouse, because the brothers paced themselves about thirty yards behind him and had no intention of drawing closer until they saw where he was headed. Officially they were hoping he might lead them to Lindy, though I have never been satisfied with that explanation. Didn't they already have a pretty good idea where she was being held? It's significant that they never hunted for her, though they knew she must be stashed within half a mile of Chester's cabin and suspected that he visited her twice a day.

So if they didn't search for her or follow him to her before this, it must have been because they had no desire to find her, either alone or in undramatic circumstances. They preferred to discover her in Chester's company, at the end of a long chase on a moonlit night, when all the trappings for a great climax were in readiness. Then they'd see if her presence might provoke Chester to some new height of delirium, securing his place in the annals of the Wilson tribe for all time.

But the brothers were not Chester's only worry as he sought to make his escape. When he drew within sight of the house, he was surprised to find that he could make out the glow of a lantern from one of the front windows, and soon he heard unexpected noises, as though a group of men or boys was singing and laughing drunkenly. Once there came the tinkling crash that glass makes when it's hurled. He entered by the back door, panting, and locked it against the Wilsons at his heels. Then he peered into the room where the voices sounded. There Chester got his next great surprise—for what he saw was Donny, pouring liquor from a stone jug into cups held out by four or five other youths. It looked at a glance as if the gang had found Grimshaw's still and had broken into this old building to hold their drunken festival. Or else they had broken in to find Lindy—who sat disdainfully in a corner, the remaining gunnysacks pulled up around her legs—and had brought along the moonshine to celebrate capturing her. Whichever way it went, they appeared well lit. One of them had already vomited across the floor in Lindy's direction. They crowed out blasphemies in the cracked voices of young manhood and sang "When you wore a tulip!" to which they had fitted bawdy lines at the end. They were not bothering with the girl for the moment, which may mean either that they had already satisfied their curiosity about her and were now drinking off their disappointment; or else they hadn't touched her yet, but were gathering courage from the jug.

One of them glimpsed Chester's form in the doorway and howled, "Here's old Chet, dressed up like a tree!"

"Come here, old Chet!" they all cried, staggering toward him, and the fat one added, "We got a cat here that wants to scratch your eyes!"

Chester backed down the hall, horrified over the desecration. They had perhaps ruined her; her cold stare hinted at that. If she was still intact, wouldn't she be screaming at these boys like a fishwife, instead of drawing into herself with pain and shame? Now he lacked the presence of mind to care about the Wilsons, who broke into the house a couple of minutes later and laid hands upon him. Seeing Lindy at the head of that trail of puke, he no longer considered it important to escape.

So, partly thanks to Donny's debauchery, Chester fell into the brothers' clutches for the final time—a circumstance I might ascribe purely to the unfailing Wilson luck, except that the chemistry of the great moment was complicated by Claude's embarrassment at finding his own son among such low companions in such a vile room. Fortunately for Claude, the confusion of seizing Chester beneath his burlap disguise provided some cover. And the joke of seeing Lindy in the boys' hands further deflected the other brothers' attention from Donny's degradation. As they marched Chester off toward Alistair's place for punishment, the other Wilsons could talk of nothing but the happy irony they detected in Lindy's fate. Though she had been the supposed prize of protracted ransom negotiations, she was now left to escape her youthful tormenters however she could. Therefore Claude was able to pretend before his brothers that he was highly pleased with his son's outrageousness. He was spared the public humiliation of having to order Donny to come along home where he belonged.

But I also know that during the next week, Claude drew

apart to worry about his son in a private, fumbling way that appeared far sadder than his distress when Kate had seemed likely to fall into Selkirk's embraces. And of course his anguish over Donny was only beginning.

For the other three brothers, though, the joy of snagging Chester was nearly pure. They had taken him exactly like they'd wanted him, looking foolish and ridiculous almost beyond belief, and in a stupid daze over his defeat. They marched the hired man across the fields toward Alistair's house, prodding him with sticks and gleefully forbidding him to take off that scratchy brown disguise which delighted them so. Originally they had voted simply to tar and feather him (their wives had been saving up chicken feathers for nearly a month), but on the inspiration of the moment they decided that parts of his burlap suit might be incorporated into a bird costume which they would force him to wear to commemorate the deaths of those hens which had lost their feet for the sake of Chester's notes.

Along the way they stopped to collect Selkirk, who writhed in a coil of ropes. The minute his gag was removed, he began to abuse Chester fiercely. "You're an archfiend out of hell and a plague of locusts and Judas Iscariot all rolled into one! May you sizzle and scorch and fry and fricassee till the grease pops out of your eyeballs and all your fingers and toes turn into solid flames! May you wander for forty days in the wilderness, and may you drown in the Red Sea with the whore of Babylon sitting on your belly to keep you under, and may the Ten Commandments fall on your noggin and smash it to smithereens!"

The brothers nearly laughed themselves sick over this spectacle, for Chester was roused out of his stupor by the preacher's shrill curses and began berating his ally for all kinds of cowardly defects, ending with his failure to hoot three times like he should have. If Chester and Selkirk had kept their wits about them, they might have even run away while the brothers were holding their sides to see one of their enemies turn upon the other with such heaven-shaking abuse.

Meanwhile back in the yard, Sophie had built a small fire to keep the tar warm, though she retreated to her kitchen when the men came up. She knew what looked seemly in a woman and had no desire to witness the tarring, so long as she could hear all the shouts and laughter through her back door.

In the stories the brothers told afterward, the climactic moment of the evening came when Claude held a lantern high and, in the ghostly light, the other brothers fitted Chester and Selkirk up like chickens, with tufts of feathers at their foreheads and elbows and butts, then forced them to cluck and scratch around the barnyard like an amorous cock and hen courting one another in a lurid dance. After a while Selkirk seemed to lose himself in the rhythm, as if strutting out some infernal message of guilt. He thrust his head back and crowed into the night air, while his elbows flapped and his shoes dragged long arcs through the dust. But Chester ducked his head to avoid visions of a black cat spitting, or of Lindy raising her horrible accusatory eyes, which he saw in every shadow. Meanwhile the Wilsons clapped hands and shook their pitchforks in the air. "Squawk, squawk!" they shouted as the man-sized birds circled the cauldron of tar.

When the brothers tired of the dance at last, they singled out Selkirk to perform a chick hatching from an egg, before hot tar was finally poured over both the captives' heads amidst a mighty bellowing of pain and outrage. My uncles swore to me, laughing uproariously, that they could not eat a drumstick for years afterward without imagining that they were biting into the preacher's thigh, so lifelike was his imitation.

In light of these high jinks, it's not surprising that both Chester and my great-uncles remembered the appearance of Johnny Acorn on the scene as a minor intrusion, an insignificant distraction for persecutors and victims alike. However, I regard his interruption as far more important than all that fowlish clowning; it seems to lead us more surely toward the real conclusion of Chester's story.

Johnny was apparently torn that night between his duties as a reporter and his obligations as a man of social conscience. On the evening when Chester and Selkirk were captured like birds of a feather, he crouched—in his reportorial capacity—behind Alistair's budding lilac bush and saw the Wilsons creep down the back steps and head off toward the creek. When the three brothers hovered near the rendezvous, overhearing the argument between Alistair and Chester, Johnny sat near them. As they closed in and then pursued the kidnapper with steady paces toward the old Douglas house, Johnny followed on tiptoe. When they penetrated the temple of Lindy's captivity, Johnny peeped through a window and strained to make out any words among the squeals and shouts. But back at Alistair's, seeing the barnyard masquerade and the flames dancing beneath the tar, he became alarmed over the news he was witnessing. Why Lindy and a bunch of drunken youths were carousing in an abandoned farmhouse he could not tell, but he could see plainly that the family which had employed Chester at no wages, neglected his welfare, and insulted his dignity was now intending to submit him, along with the local Methodist clergyman, to a kind of vigilante persecution which smacked more of witch burnings than the modern rule of law. Johnny could print this outrage tomorrow—indeed, he intended to—but didn't he also have a responsibility to confront the tyrants on their own turf? Which is what he did.

The Wilson brothers were much too surprised over the pesky newspaperman's appearance to attend much to what he said, and they were too delighted over the prospect of the further punishment they were about to inflict on Chester and the preacher to be in a mood for conversation. Before Johnny could finish his protest, they began taunting him, "You want a feather tail yourself, you bird-nose? Or how about a squirt of tar in your ears?"

If he had been more observant, Johnny might have noticed that even Chester, his supposed comrade in the class struggle, found his speech laughable. In later years Chester always described Johnny as a fool and a half for believing any stranger's words could turn the Wilsons from their revenge. At last the brothers simply ignored him, taking up Selkirk again for the application of some good-natured pitch. When Johnny threatened, "I'm going to write this up and expose you to the world!" they laughed again. Their mood had mounted so high that fear of the press, which had intimidated them earlier, now flew from their minds. They would soon care quite a bit about the story Johnny would write, but on the crucial night they could not focus on it, their imaginations were so exalted with their victory.

Unable to influence the course of events, Johnny at last stalked to his car, leaving the rest of the evening's news unobserved. He had already seen all he needed for his article, and had stored up enough indignation to carry him through another month of reporting about the Wilsons.

Chapter Nine

Old Stewart must have liked Johnny's report well enough, because he printed it in full beneath a two-column headline on the front page. Still, I imagine that some confusion must have mingled with the editor's pride, because the piece did not read exactly as he and Lawyer Beagle were expecting. Johnny had been sent out to cover a kidnapping, but the headline read, "Vigilante Outrage by Local Farmers!"

When I showed this article to Chester once, he was vastly amused, since it completely vindicated his side of the quarrel. There was only one mention of "an alleged but unproven snatch" in the next-to-last paragraph. All the rest described how youths and middle-aged men ran in packs on our road, terrorizing any weaklings who fell in their way. Stewart apparently did not possess a fine ear for nuance, since he let his reporter get away with a couple of references to "agricultural bossism" and "the rural proletariat." But at least Johnny was not antichurch, for his depiction of Selkirk the Martyr was sympathetic. I assume this was an attempt to placate the religious scruples of his readership by showing that Christianity in its most heroic hours stands on the side of the underdog.

Johnny's article was one of the few cases when the Wilsons found themselves anticipated in storytelling, because the paper came out on Saturday, one day ahead of their first chance to spread the news among their cronies after Sunday services. I would like to know how they handled themselves in the churchyard before an audience whose minds had already been poisoned by a rival version of the tale, but they always refused to discuss that episode with me.

Ordinary townspeople and farmers were not the only ones influenced by Johnny's article, of course. Lots of folks read the Hickman *Sun,* including the sheriff and the regional news editor of the Saint Joe *Gazette.* If the brothers had momentarily forgotten the power of the press when they laughed Johnny off our road, they were reminded of it painfully on Monday morning, when two cars pulled into Alistair's driveway and a couple of men wearing city slicker suits knocked at the front door. My great-uncles brushed off all my questions about this episode too, claiming it only amounted to some pointless snooping by people who didn't have enough business of their own. But Chester told me that Sophie called Alistair up from the barn right away, and he stood talking in the side yard for well over an hour, unable to shake the outsiders off.

Chester was watching the interrogation from the window of his cabin. He had ceased to work for Alistair after the night he was nabbed and punished. Alistair, on his side, had stopped dispatching meals down to his former employee. Chester was nursing several bad bruises and possibly a cracked rib, though his main concern was to clean off the remains of the tarring. He had already applied nearly a gallon of stolen gasoline as a solvent—rubbing large patches of skin raw—and had cut off big swatches of his hair, yet when he looked into the tin mirror propped on his table, he still saw wide spots of black about his face and neck, hands and arms. He was afraid to hit the road looking that way, because the fellows who rode the boxcars were an observant lot. They could size up another man in a single glance, and they might just as likely feel merciless as sympathetic toward anyone who'd gotten himself tarred and run out of town. Chester was hoping that by late in the week he'd be ready to travel; in the meantime he'd like to see any Wilson try to chase him out of that cabin!

After an inconclusive coversation with Alistair, the two city-suited men inquired where the hired man was. Reluctantly Alistair led them to Chester's door and knocked. When Chester, who was instinctively reluctant to show himself while he looked so mottled, finally opened up a crack and stuck out his long nose, Alistair spoke before either the Saint Joe reporter or the deputy sheriff could open his mouth. He said, "Now *think careful* before you answer any questions, or these fellows'll make some mistake about you and me both!"

Chester quickly saw what Alistair meant. It would've been easy for him to say, "Sure, Mr. Wilson tarred and feathered us. He's kept me on for a year without wages. He's knocked me in the head once or twice to boot." In that case all the brothers might have stood before a judge—an outcome that was all the more likely because the newspaper publicity had created pressure on the sheriff's office to act, though Chester only found out about that angle later. Anyway, the Wilsons' arrest would decisively interrupt the family's long string of victories, and it might even help unravel the mystery of how Alistair got his hands on somebody else's eighty acres. But Chester also saw how much more he had to lose than the Wilsons, for he had read about dozens of snatch cases and he knew perfectly well that the legal penalty for a conviction was the chair. So he stammered, "I've worked for Mr. Wilson eleven months. I only see the Methodist preacher in church— he's one hell of a talker, isn't he? But no, we weren't ever chased around half the countryside at night, nor had hot tar poured over our heads. That must've been somebody else."

The deputy and the reporter looked disappointed, especially because they could see the splotchy black map of his persecution written all over Chester. They asked why his ears were filled with pitch and his hair snipped off. Alistair remarked from the background, "I told them about your accident, but they wouldn't believe me." The story was going to be that Chester'd been repairing a shed roof when he'd lost his balance, pulling the can of pitch along on top of his head.

"Yep," said Chester as soon as he understood, "that's what I did."

The deputy and the reporter were not easily satisfied, but finally they exhausted their ingenuity and drove away in their separate cars. Neither of them thought to ask which shed Chester had been repairing, and by the time the sheriff drove out on Tuesday to pursue the investigation his deputy had botched, Alistair had climbed onto a roof and spread some tar around in a half-convincing pattern of spill and fall. But two new elements, which Alistair had not calculated on, intervened to throw this interview in the sheriff's favor. Johnny Acorn came along to help with the questioning, because he could not understand why Chester had denied suffering any wrong. At this point Johnny must have been fired not only by a passion for social justice, but also by his desire to prove the truth of his big news story. When Alistair and Chester saw the sheriff's black sedan pull into the driveway, they felt their hearts sink a little, but when they saw Johnny tumble out of the passenger side, breathlessly calling to Chester, "What's this, what's this, did he threaten you? Is he paying you off?" both men gasped in horror.

Still, so much was at stake that they had to make the effort to keep up their lie. As soon as the sheriff drew within hearing, Alistair began repeating his story, with Chester looking desperately at the horizon and mumbling "Yeah" whenever Alistair prodded him for confirmation. The sheriff's eyes narrowed to suspicious slits and Johnny ran a brutal cross-examination, but so long as Chester held firm the law could do nothing. Thus Alistair might have gotten rid of the interlopers at last—except that in his desire to convince the sheriff, my uncle offered, "Come on down and see the roof old Chester slipped from."

There was the black streak running down the shingles, there was the carefully planted bucket of tar in the weeds, there was the brush lying conspicuously beside it, but there was also an unexpected rustle from deeper in the thick spring grasses growing in that deserted corner, and after a minute up like a slender hollyhock stood Lindy, her latest hiding place discovered.

The sheriff and Johnny Acorn surely had no idea what to make of her. Johnny's earlier news story indicates that he had glimpsed her among the carousing boys when he peered in the old farmhouse window, so he knew she might have important evidence to give, but he seems not to have credited the kidnapping rumor much, so her role in the story must have been a mystery to him. But as she wavered above the knee-high verdure in her grimy nightgown, Alistair and Chester both felt their cases come to judgment. For Alistair it was simply the problem of a new witness whose testimony he could not control, but Chester's shock arose from regarding Lindy as the symbol of all his guilt and foolishness. After he beheld her fleetingly on the night he was tarred and feathered, his love for her was suspended in an apprehension that because of him, she had been ruined. She became a thing of the past—an object he had destroyed out of greed and a stupid desire for revenge. Thus his impulse was to avoid her, as a small boy tries to hide from an accusatory finger, and it had not even occurred to him to return the next morning, while the tar was still fresh in his hair, to see if she remained in the abandoned farmhouse. He gazed at her now immobilized by shame, and waited for lightning to strike him down.

The sheriff, a red-haired beefy fellow named McLean, had driven out to Alistair's place intending to act decisively for the benefit of the reporter he brought along, so he grabbed the girl's slender arm and shook her when she seemed unable to speak. Alistair was trying to attract her attention with hand signals. But she seemed to have lost the power of concentration; she only rattled her head and leaned at an angle away from the sheriff, until water was brought and she was placed on a milking stool and the questions were repeated slowly. Finally her eyes focused and she nodded cryptically, "They did it." After that she slumped back, leaving the sheriff and Johnny scratching their heads.

Now the sheriff stamped around the barnyard in frustration for a minute and then drew some quick conclusions based on appearances. He had noticed that when Lindy stood up amid the weeds unexpectedly, Alistair lost all his stuffing and took on the look of a criminal. He had seen that although Chester confirmed Alistair's story, the hired man's face told an opposite tale, and when Lindy appeared, Chester seemed to melt with solicitousness and ran to fetch the water and the stool for her. The tar-and-feathering was probably true, then, and in spite of what the reporter believed, there might have been a kidnapping too. If so, Alistair was the most likely perpetrator, and the sheriff determined he would have a better chance of extracting a confession if he threw the suspect in jail to break his spirit. After Lindy spoke, therefore, it took only a minute for the handcuffs to appear. Alistair, who had been relieved to find that Lindy had lost her senses, was too surprised by this sudden turn to protest much. He was led across the barnyard and thrown into the car, leaving Lindy still hunched on the milking stool and Chester standing distractedly before her.

My uncles never spoke of Alistair's arrest, of course. For them, Chester's history ceased abruptly after he and the preacher were tarred. So I am forced to depend entirely on Chester's account, except for certain paragraphs from the next two issues of the *Sun*, which record a few bare, insufficient facts. The newspaper fails to mention that on a Tuesday morning in early May, two of the poorest underlings in the county, who didn't own a scrap of land between them, succeeded, without speaking more than ten words, in causing proud Alistair Wilson to be arrested, to his family's everlasting shame. Chester and Lindy might have celebrated that great revenge by turning cartwheels over the chicken house or torching the barn before they skipped off into the clouds. But as I have cut through Chester's blurry version of this decisive moment it has become clear that he and the girl were so stupefied with exhaustion and fear that neither of them realized their victory. Not until Sophie appeared at the kitchen door and called, "Where'd they take my man to?" did Chester come to himself enough to comprehend that Alistair was gone.

After that, he first expected the sheriff to return before nightfall and arrest him too, as soon as Alistair made it plain that if he had been guilty of a little roughhousing, Chester was the kidnapper. It didn't occur to him that the sheriff still had no evidence except Johnny Acorn's confused account of an event he didn't understand, and consequently there was no reason for Alistair to switch stories just because he had been taken to jail. So the fear still gripped Chester, and he might simply have stood dithering, or hid in some ditch—had not Sophie, on her way to hitch the team so she could ride down and tell the other Wilsons the shocking news, yelled at Chester, "Get that slut off the farm before I get back, or there'll be hell to pay!"

Her shrill command caused him to focus on Lindy for the first time, not as a piece of proof against himself or as a remote image of pathos, but as the girl he had stolen because he loved her. He suddenly burned with the desire to bring her back to life if he could. He walked over to her while Sophie was still hitching up the horses and extended his hand. Lindy looked up and realized at once that he meant to treat her right. Delicately she grasped his fingers and raised herself from the stool. Then she took his arm and limped beside him down to the cabin, not speaking a word.

They had established a housekeeping routine of sorts during the kidnapping. They were used to each other's breathing and to the particular smell of each other's clothes. They had depended on one another in a host of ways for several weeks, so it is not surprising that once inside Chester's cabin, they fell by habit into an intense domesticity, even though their previous relationship had often been quarrelsome and frustrating. Lindy's spunk had been knocked out of her, and as she slowly gathered her wits together, she must have faced the truth that beyond Chester's cabin, she had nowhere to go except a mythical place called California, where they probably didn't want her anyway.

Chester described those thirty-six hours they spent together in the cabin as a chaste honeymoon, a temporary reprieve from the expected knock on the door that would mean the electric chair was waiting for him. Like some old Hollywood hero sent to death row by mistake, he pretended not to care, because his beloved had come to pay a last visit to his cell. He and Lindy hardly spoke during all that time they were closed up together. She was faint and maybe traumatized, but she came back to life slowly once Chester got her inside the little room and tried to arrange things for her comfort.

They heard Sophie drive back at nightfall. She brought along Donny's younger brother Horace to do the milking, since Chester was no longer considered to work for the family. Chester waited until all fell quiet again outside and then he slipped down to the henhouse and snared one more sleeping chicken for Lindy's dinner. His return with the bird seemed to rouse the girl more than anything else had. After he plucked and gutted it, she roasted it over a little fire of twigs, and as she and her protector sat down to eat, she showed her first tentative smile. It was at this point, I believe, that Chester decided she remained pure in spite of Donny and his gang. Her expression lingered afterward in his memory as a hint that his own guilt was not so great as he had feared, and that reprieve fueled his adoration.

She slept in Chester's bed of corncobs and rags, while he lay on the floor beside her wrapped in his coat, his mind racing over thoughts of prison and the chair—though as the hours passed he began to wonder why the sheriff had not come. He hardly dared to think that if he played his cards right, he might achieve his desires after all. He still could not believe that luck was turning decisively against the Wilsons at last. And yet he was still free, while Alistair was in jail!

The next morning he dropped some hints to Lindy about the brighter possibilities that might be before them, and maybe that brief conversation was what caused her to decide to bank on Chester totally. Anyway, the most intriguing fact in this part of the tale is that somehow her mind gradually evolved from its daze into the clear purposefulness she displayed the next night, when the remaining Wilson brothers showed up at Chester's cabin to cajole him into helping them free Alistair from the sheriff. I would like to have asked Lindy how she began to accept the idea that Chester was her man and she would stand by him. Could he have ceased to look ridiculous at last, and become her silver screen lover? Or did she suddenly grow up during those hours alone with him inside the cabin, and realize that only by clinging to him might she get the chance to utter a punch line of her own which would confound her betters?

When the three brothers tapped at the cabin door, Chester thought the law had finally come for him, but he recovered from his fright in time to keep them standing at a disadvantage, outside in the dark. At first Lindy only peeped out at them from below his armpit. Claude broke the silence, staring up at Chester's soupy black and white face. "They got your boss in the county jail, you know."

Chester countered that one. "Not my boss. I quit."

"He's your boss and we're all your bosses and we will be until we let you go. You're living in our cabin. Don't you forget that. We got something on you that the law'll be happier than a cricket to find out about. If you don't come into town and tell them there wasn't any tar-and-feathering, Alistair'll break the word about the kidnapping."

Chester was much relieved to hear that Alistair hadn't pointed any blame at him yet, but he had no clear idea how much of an advantage he now held over the Wilsons, if any. Besides, the case had become so serious—with the fear of execution hanging over him—that Chester was no longer thinking of fencing gamely with the brothers. Yet the gift of gab remained instinctive, and as he struggled for air he started bluffing to see how far he could go. He and Lindy had reached no explicit agreement, but he gambled that she would back him up.

"What proof you got of any kidnapping?" he began.

"You know blame well what proof we got! Alistair met you by the dark of the moon to turn over a deed for the ransom, and we chased you right to where you were keeping the gal. We'll all four swear to it, and your goose'll be cooked."

"What if the gal says she wasn't snatched?" he asked, and suddenly the brothers looked past him and saw the face within the cabin and realized what had happened with Lindy. Again they were forced to confront the mystery of her sex. They must have felt a tingling premonition that the outcome of their struggle with Chester was now incalculable. Doubtless Claude regretted that he had not seen the necessity of taking the girl back among them and treating her like family, to secure her testimony. But he had to find out how much Chester could deliver, so he spoke to the face inside.

"You wouldn't be such a fool, would you, gal? You were kidnapped for sure, you know you were. Because if you weren't, you were helping this weasel extort land from us, which is almost as bad a crime as kidnapping. They send gals like you to the pen for telling lies just as quick as they send the menfolks."

Chester had not anticipated the new charge of extortion and did not know how to meet it. When he told this story, he was generous enough to abandon all claim to the gab after a certain point, in order to give Lindy credit for the quick wit that saved him.

What she told Claude, looking him pretty straight in the eye, was, "Your boy raped me. Him and his friends. What you think the law's going to say about that?"

In the silence that fell over the Wilson brothers, the stars seemed to fall from their appointed places and a curve was notched in our road where it had run straight before. As well as I recall my great-uncles' faces, I cannot picture how shocked or deflated they must have looked at this moment—maybe like nothing more than pale bladders of empty air. Anyway, Claude saw there was nothing more to be tried, no more lies to be told. Still he couldn't resist one more half-hearted effort. He told Lindy, "You come home with me, little gal. My wife'll see to you. You need a bath and a clean bed. You've suffered enough. No use of you staying out here in this stinking cabin with white trash when you're family to us."

Chester endured an anxious moment when he heard this invitation, but she was not tempted. "I wouldn't rest under your roof with that boy around. He might break into my room. I'm safer here than I would be anywhere else."

"Yeah," said Chester, recovering. "She's got her own man to take care of her now. She doesn't need any other family but me."

Lindy's fate was settled then and Claude could only supplicate. What tone must his voice have taken on as he said, "You aren't planning to leave your boss in jail and testify against him, are you? You wouldn't accuse my Donny to the sheriff and ruin his young life?"

"It'd be a crying shame," Jethro threw in. "A boy carted off for having a little fun and not meaning harm. Why, he'd never come back to his ma alive if they took him away on a charge like that."

Chester began to savor his position, and he saw no reason to hold back. "I understand Mr. Alistair's going to put those eighty acres on the market tomorrow," he said. "Including Miss Lindy's old farmhouse. I'll give him fifty cents for the lot."

The silence descended once more as the Wilsons took this in. Jethro may have started to say something angry, but Claude nudged him back. "Sold!" he muttered. "Let's go home, boys. We'll pick you two up bright and early tomorrow and run you into town, first to the jail to clear Alistair and then to the lawyer's for the deed of sale."

"First the deed and then the jail," Chester called after them as they hunched into a pack and moved away from the cabin's light into the darkness. And the way he said it was the way it was. Alistair, who found every hour under the sheriff's thumb a fresh humiliation, was left to cool his heels until four o'clock the next afternoon, while Chester dawdled over papers in Bill Beagle's office and then somehow forced Claude to treat him and Lindy to a celebratory fried lunch at the Sunnyside Cafe. Riding home that evening in the back seat of Claude's bulky old car between two of his brothers, Alistair buried his face in his hands. No one spoke during the trip, though up front Chester hugged Lindy openly, and from the back came a short, dry wheezing that might have been the sound of a Wilson gasping for breath.

Donny's disappearance from our road remains a family mystery. Did his father hustle him away in case Lindy should voice her charges again once she and Chester gained possession of the eighty acres? Or was the boy so distraught at hearing she was going to marry Chester that he took to the open road in hopes of forgetting her? Anyway, a couple of mornings after the deed was signed and Alistair was released, while news of a prospective wedding was circulating among the farmhouses beyond the Wilsons, Kate was surprised to see that her elder son did not come down as usual to help with the milking. He did not appear at breakfast. He was not in his bedroom. His brother Horace had heard no sounds during the night. His school friends, when Claude telephoned them—either in a genuine search for information or as a way of covering his son's tracks—claimed to know nothing about Donny's plans. The neighboring fields were searched, and Tony helped Claude wade through a frigid pond where boys played in the summers, just in case a bloated body was floating in it, though everyone knew the weather was still too raw for Donny to have gone for a swim. By week's end the parents were admitting among the family that their son had run away. Kate was seen to wipe a few tears, and Claude's mouth was tightly set. No note was ever found, and the rest of the Wilsons never heard of any letter. Claude buried the subject with as few words as he could.

A more joyous departure that spring was Selkirk's, which occurred about two weeks later and was made festive by the marriage over which he presided on the Saturday before he left town. He had served to the end of his purgatorial Hickman year, and the bishop dispatched him next to Lexington, a town fifty miles distant. He would probably have preferred some more remote corner of the state, but he was glad enough simply to be leaving. His final sermon was based on the liberation of the Chosen People from Egypt and their safe passage across the Red Sea, to the dismay of the Pharaoh's pursuing army. He did not stand by the church door to shake hands afterward; the Model A was packed and waiting for him in a side street. There is no proof he ever thought about Sophie again, and if in later years she indulged any idle memories, she kept her own counsel.

On his way out of town Selkirk must have chuckled with satisfaction over the way Chester and Lindy's wedding had turned out, for its raucous climax amounted to a rejection of all those pieties the church had blamed him for letting down. None of the Wilsons attended the ceremony, of course, although my grandfather swore that he was eager to go, after Chester walked down the road one afternoon and invited him—partly in recognition that Grandpa was the one man in the family who'd treated him decently, and partly in hopes of starting a feud, I expect. But my grandma refused to accompany him, being a loyal Wilson, and threatened, "Just you try to go without me!"

So the guest list was confined to distant acquaintances of the groom, although it did contain some surprises: Bill Beagle sat up front, dressed in a solemn dark suit but quite likely smiling to himself for reasons Chester didn't suspect. Old Grimshaw the bootlegger stood by the rear door, waiting for the reception which was to follow the ceremony. Word had spread like a prairie fire among the neighborhood farmhands. None of them knew Chester well, but all were curious to see one of their own get hitched, especially because he was marrying that pretty girl they had stared at every week during Selkirk's sermons.

The preacher had reconciled with Chester by this time, despite the indignities he had suffered because of the kidnapping. Like everyone else he was ignorant of the means, but he knew the hired man had gained those eighty acres at last, and he was tickled pink over the Wilsons' final defeat. He beamed at the bride and groom across his Bible, he offered a brief sermon on the sacred pleasures of intimacy between male and female with eye-twitching gusto, and he pronounced the vows in his best sepulchral voice. Despite these signs of grace, Chester was still surprised at the end of the service when Selkirk told him, "This one's on the house!" Chester recognized that for the miracle it was, but in the exuberance of the moment he pressed a couple of quarters into the preacher's hand regardless.

The marriage didn't make the Hickman *Sun*'s society page. I have checked thoroughly. So it is impossible to recover what Lindy looked like or how she acted on that day. Chester's story of his wedding is virtually useless, since he remembered the affair in a kind of golden, perfumed haze. Where did the young bride get her white dress and veil, I wonder, with no family to provide for her, no girlfriends in the surrounding county, or even a schoolteacher who might have rememberd her fondly and treated her, for the occasion, like a daughter? Did she even find shoes to wear? More to the point, did she rest against Chester's side at the altar, eager to cherish, honor, and obey? Or was a sly smile playing about her lips?

Years later Chester did remember the tender brief kiss when they were pronounced man and wife, but I must use my own imagination to describe the way the guests hustled downstairs to the basement afterward, where two great glass bowls, used for temperance punches at church socials, sat on a rickety folding table next to a stack of dainty cups. There was no cake, but the bowls brimmed with a reeking brown liquid in which floated a few apple slices. Old man Grimshaw took up a ladle and began dispensing the cheer. The farmhands quickly forgot the newlyweds and pressed around to be served. Bill Beagle, curious and grinning, stood in line with the others. Even Johnny Acorn, who had dropped by uninvited to look things over, accepted a cup. But the farmhands were not accustomed to such a treat, and in a noisy good-humored half hour they drained both bowls, toasting

"Good old Chet!" and "To the new little Missus!" Finally they smashed the cups on the concrete floor when the liquor ran out.

By this time Bill Beagle had crept away and Chester had rescued his bride from the hullabaloo, and set out with her on foot for their newly acquired property. It was not much of a wedding journey, perhaps, hand in hand down a dirt road past the farmhouses of their enemies. But the Wilsons made it less objectionable by turning their backs: nobody came down to the road to jeer. Shades were pulled at the windows in the middle of the afternoon. If Chester and Lindy thought they could make it alone in the world, the Wilsons were telling them, then let them find out how alone they really were!

Back at the church, Selkirk could see how the drunken farmhands were fulfilling the promise of Grimshaw's brew by smashing the folding furniture and glassware, but he must have simply smirked and disappeared too. He had no sentimental reason to protect church property in Hickman; he was leaving for good tomorrow anyway. Only Johnny Acorn remained to observe that the mob, after it cracked the sacred punch bowls to much joyous hooting, surged up the stairs and into the street where young men picked up stones and hurled them through the front windows of houses as they passed on their way toward the business district. They sang and howled like dogs. They were planning to storm the Wall Brothers' drygoods store—perhaps inspired by the thought of all those paint cans they might slosh around—until they were met by the local police chief and his deputy, both nervously pointing rifles at the sky. After that the farmhands calmed down pretty quickly, and in twos and threes they made for side streets and slipped into the country lanes without being followed. The shocked townspeople gathered in the street then, nearly silent, looking at the broken glass but not comprehending what had hit them in the middle of a peaceful spring afternoon, until one or two repeated, "It was that Chester's wedding party!" Others nodded; that seemed to explain it all. But as might be expected, Johnny Acorn reported the story from his own angle the next Tuesday. His tall black headline read, "Farm Workers Rise In Protest! Look Out Chicago: Hickman Has Unrest Too!"

By the time this article appeared Chester and Lindy had already finished sweeping out the empty warped rooms of their old unpainted house and were setting into the fields for the spring planting, their seed grain having been obtained on credit like a lot of other folks', their plow the rusty bent implement Lindy's father had abandoned in a shed when he gave up and moved. To pull it, Chester borrowed a swaybacked mule from some neighbor both kinder and more distant than the Wilsons. The neighbor had agreed partly because the mule wasn't good for much anyway, and partly because he was amused over the rumor that Chester had somehow pried those acres away from Alistair against his will. A couple of farm wives brought Lindy some flour and lard and dried beans in the same spirit. Pretty soon Chester understood that many folks in the vicinity would help him and his new wife get by until the harvest, mainly because it was good to have them settled there as a buffer between the Wilsons and the rest of the human race.

When I was a boy everybody in the family understood that the art of storytelling depends mostly on knowing how to quit. As I watched my great-uncles—hoary old men by the time I knew them—sitting on a porch in the summer evenings, spinning their yarns about Chester's first year on our road, I observed that no matter how far the narrative might ramble or how many interruptions the listeners threw in, the whole performance was invariably saved by the way the teller delivered his climax. Just before he reached the punch line, he would begin to chuckle, signaling that the end was near. When he finally spoke it, his voice would speed up and the pitch would rise, preparatory to knee-slapping and guffawing. The last words would sound as inevitable as a poem. Everyone in the circle felt the achievement at that moment: they loved the way all the strands came together quick and clean.

That's why I'm stopping here, with Chester's wedding and the disappearance of Donny, with Alistair brought home from jail in his shame and Sophie madder than a wet hen over her skinny young cousin marrying to escape taking orders from her betters, and all of Hickman thinking Chester was a crazy wild fellow to have such a wedding, but admiring his vague suspected triumph over the Wilsons anyway. The last image hovering over my story should be Chester grinning in his wry, crooked way as he remembered those days of his victory and his love, coming together by glorious chance when he had given up on both.

Down on my grandfather's farm, where Chester told me his version of things to counter the stories my great-uncles preferred, it always seemed that his life had indeed ended then, with his young wife under her sunbonnet walking toward him over their own fields. Afterward, it was as though Chester had been forced to live beyond his time, as if he had become a minor figure in somebody else's story instead, one he wasn't much interested in and only tolerated. Lindy never fully regained her strength after the kidnapping. Something never felt right down below, and when she gave birth the first winter after their marriage, the child was stillborn. Her frailty showed in the way she kept house. My great-aunts, who never stepped foot inside the place, insisted the cobwebs hung like broad curtains, and even Chester admitted that she never improved much as a cook. Meanwhile he found the eighty acres too small a spread to turn much profit on, even though the rains had returned and the countryside grew thick green in the springs again. Besides, while he had learned certain farming skills from the Wilsons, he had been so preoccupied with undermining Alistair's operations that he hadn't bothered to find out about rotating crops or figuring expenses or a hundred other things, and his pride prevented him from asking questions of the neighbors who might have given sound advice. What's more, there are seasons on a farm when one man just isn't enough, when he needs a brother or a son to help, and Lindy, willing as she might have been, lacked the strength to lift a forkful of hay. She could barely carry in the water she needed for the kitchen, and every winter she seemed to weaken a degree more.

Finally one frosty afternoon my grandpa couldn't bear any longer to think about the two of them scrabbling in their poverty, while the farmers on all sides were prospering again. He drove down to visit Chester and ended up telling him, "There's no sense of you sitting on this land half-starving. Sell it back to Alistair and come work for me."

Grandpa told me how he and Chester looked across the room at Lindy, who sat wrapped in a shawl, her cheeks hollow, her eyes closed in a way that hinted she even slept with pain, and it was clear to both men that before long Chester would be alone on his farm, with no one to cook or wash or mind the kitchen garden.

Yet when Chester first approached Alistair about buying back the eighty acres, he was told, "I'll give you fifty cents, just the price you bought it for!"

At once Chester regretted that he had come over to a Wilson's front porch looking like a beggar, and snorted, "Lots of other neighbors might want to strike a deal if you don't." Then he stomped back to his house in disgust.

But the way the land lay, Alistair was clearly the logical buyer, and after a couple of weeks he found the temptation to expand his holdings again irresistible, especially since two of his boys were now old enough to help work the land. Even after he'd signaled his interest, though, he took his time coming to terms, and it would be easy to imagine the two opponents falling once more into an endless maze of negotiations as Alistair angled for a chance at revenge. This time, though, my grandpa stepped in to mediate, and then Chester brought his invalid wife down to live in a little cabin beyond my grandfather's barn.

I should stress that my great-uncles played no part in Chester's decision to sell out. They proved not to be such a nuisance to his farming as you might expect. Mostly they just ignored him. Though they always loved to talk about Chester afterward, it seems that for them the final Chester-story ended with the tar-and-feathering, and they never had the stomach to try to arrange any new ones. When Alistair came home from jail he was visibly shaken. He had defied all the sheriff's efforts to force a confession, but the humiliation of being in anybody else's power for forty-eight hours was a cruel new experience, made worse by the disgust his brothers and his wife showed toward him in the weeks afterward. Sophie ruled the roost now, calling her husband "You stupid ninny!" for not thinking fast enough to escape the law's clutches. His brothers shunned him for a season, as though they were trying to redesign the family tree with Alistair's branch lopped off. He made no attempt to redeem himself in their eyes. He sat alone by his kitchen stove night after night all the following year, and even when his wife raised her voice in abuse, he never answered back. Long afterward, he remained slighter, shyer than his brothers. When I knew him in my boyhood, he would occasionally recount a story, but mostly he just laughed at other folks'.

Consequently none of the Wilsons were in peak condition to launch a new assault against Chester after he took possession of his land, although maybe their inaction was partly strategic too: they could have been simply waiting for his venture at farming to fail on its own, as they were pretty sure it would have to. But for my uncles' sake I would like to think that Alistair's shame forced them all to consider certain chastening truths. I would like to think they saw how, during Chester's first year, they had descended from practical jokes and an occasional swindle to a level of cunning cruelty which was unworthy of the family name. I would like to believe they understood at last the dangers of story-arranging—they who had always relied on luck to enhance their gift of gab, who had thought they could always hurl themselves into the swirling elements and emerge with the conclusion of their choice in hand. Luck was perhaps the most fascinating element in existence to them, and yet so little did they understand it that until the very moment of Johnny Acorn's appearance, none of them realized their luck was capable of such a double-cross as tossing the reporter into their midst.

With his profit on the sale, Chester opened a bank account for the first time in his life, though finally most of the money was spent to keep Lindy comfortable for the time she had left. I grew up watching him sow and reap, feed and slaughter under my grandfather's direction, and in the evening he whittled and smoked and told his tales to whoever would listen. Often he and Grandpa would take off fishing for an afternoon when my grandmother's back was turned. My grandpa didn't tell many stories himself, but he enjoyed some of Chester's pretty well.

I have wondered if the struggle was worth it, since Chester ended up as he'd begun, a hired hand jumping to another man's whistle. He apologized to my grandmother whenever she scolded (which was pretty often), slept alone and, except for the stories, kept his thoughts to himself. Once I asked, with the bluntness of a child, if the Wilsons hadn't beaten him after all?

He raised his eyes from the cigarette he was rolling and I could tell that my question had roused something in him. "You never met her, son. You couldn't know. Every time I close my eyes, her pure face is lying on the pillow beside me. That's something none of those Wilsons can say."

Now when I picture him and Lindy walking up the little rise behind their farmhouse, from which they could survey the land with a fierce, proud gleam of victory and possession, I sometimes suspect there was another reason the brothers stopped meddling with Chester after the wedding: because a fellow may live among stories for months or years, while chance buffets him with its droll punch lines, but then in an instant a fresh tide may sweep away all the condescending laughter and there he'll be, washed up on a distant, wondrous shore where no teller of tales can touch him.